The
Psychic Vampire

The
Psychic Vampire

DR. THOMAS E. BERRY

iUniverse, Inc.
Bloomington

The Psychic Vampire

iUniverse books may be ordered through booksellers or by contacting:

iUniverse
1663 Liberty Drive
Bloomington, IN 47403
www.iuniverse.com
1-800-Authors (1-800-288-4677)

Author Credits: Two previous books chosen for Editors Choice

ISBN: 978-1-4620-2898-6 (sc)
ISBN: 978-1-4620-2897-9 (ebk)

Library of Congress Control Number: 2011909736

Printed in the United States of America

iUniverse rev. date: 06/10/2011

CONTENTS

Chapter 1

The Cemetery

Last night I overcame my fear and visited her grave. I admit that I entered the cemetery with trepidation and walked among the dark, ancient oak trees with anxiety. As I moved toward the family plot, it seemed that the gnarled and twisted limbs in the darkness above were bending down menacingly toward me. Yet I knew that I must assure myself that she could no longer harm me. As I approached the great stone monuments that declared the past glories of others, moonlight made ghastly shadows around me through the boughs of the trees. I shuddered.

Then suddenly I was standing before her grave. She did not come out of her tomb and grab my leg as I had envisioned. That sort of vampire is in ghost stories and literature. When she was alive, she never had teeth that would sink into her victim's neck as did the legendary fiends so named. No, she was a beautiful woman capable of far worse torture than the spilling of blood, and her venom still exudes from the depths of her hell. Even from her coffin the vengeful acts she perpetrated while alive continue to extend misery to those who tried to love her. Encased within her were demons far worse than any storied horror. She was not nourished by human blood but survived on human minds. She was a psychic vampire.

It was the power of her eyes that did it. One piercing look from those large, dark, beckoning eyes caused an inner fear to instantly seize a person and cause them to submit to her power. Her long, lustrous brunette hair heightened her perfect facial features, yet her beauty was deceiving. Anyone who met her for the first time could easily say that she was one of the sweetest, kindest, and loveliest mortals they had ever encountered. And she could be. How easily her smile captivated, and how kindly she could express herself. If she wanted, she could win over the heart of anyone. It was, as she would say, "the Jesus way" that propelled her.

No one has ever used the holy name of Christ more cleverly and more intentionally. She claimed that He was with her all the time. He was her companion, her beloved, her Savior. Using His name, she entrapped her victims. I could not understand why a God would allow such a creature to so misuse His power, but she ruled in her world of hatred and envy by hiding behind the beauty and solace of eternal wisdom: Peace on earth, good will to men!

I remember very well when she came into my life. The spring semester at Lake Forest College had just ended, and I had driven home in my canary-yellow convertible. I parked by the rose garden of our home near Lake Michigan. Near our house, my mother was sitting with Slep, our collie, in a gazebo surrounded by redbud trees. I waved and walked over to her.

After patting the family pet, I kissed my mother; but when she thanked me, I sensed a tenseness in her voice. She was excited because my older brother John was bringing his girlfriend to meet our family. I knew this was a special event for her, because we knew how badly she wanted her oldest son to settle down. He had left college during his first year in order to join the US Army. He wanted adventure.

After he returned from two years in Iraq, he seemed restless, as if he did not know what to do with himself. He drank beer with former high school football buddies, and he worked continually on his car, but he lounged before the TV for long hours. He had spent his time in the military as a sergeant overseeing military supplies in a warehouse. Mother assumed that he missed being so active. Now he was involved with a girlfriend, and that could mean marriage. My mother's hopes were at last being fulfilled. I was happy for her.

"Tom, dear," she said to me as we walked through the garden to the sunroom entrance of our home, "would you do me a favor this evening?"

"Of course, Mother," I replied, holding her hand.

"Please don't talk about religion during dinner. I know how you love to upset me with your irreligious banter, but don't tease me this evening. Will you?"

"Of course," I responded, stopping to hug her. "You know I'd do anything to make you happy."

She thanked me.

"I take it that she's a religious type?"

"I don't know for sure, but John sort of asked that we not talk about our church this evening."

I laughed as we walked across the patio to the sunroom. "Well, I'll try to behave, but if she's going to cram Jesus down my throat, I might say something."

Mother halted as she put a lock of her graying hair back into the bun behind her head. "Tom, you hurt me when you mention Christ so nonchalantly. Why do you taunt me that way?"

I opened one of the French doors to the sunroom and said, "Oh, Mother, dear, let's not get off on that old argument now. Let's be happy."

Mother smiled. "Yes, I am happy, but I do have a dilemma."

As we sat down on a wicker couch near the many-paned windows of the sunroom, I petted Slep again and asked, "What do you mean?"

"Well, my oldest son seems to be settling down," she commented as she smoothed a wrinkle from her silk paisley skirt, "while my middle son is drifting away!"

"Where am I drifting?" I asked.

Mother smiled. "Oh, let's not start. We'll talk about you another time. In a few minutes, I've got things to do in the kitchen. I want to just sit a moment and enjoy this lovely spring day. You can help by starting the fire in the family room."

And so, preparations for the great occasion took our thoughts away from her so-called dilemma. As I cleaned the ashes out of our large brick fireplace, I thought of Mother and how happy she would be if her oldest son finally settled down. She would undoubtedly be very generous in helping the young couple with finances, because she had the thought of a grandchild constantly on her mind. I also wondered what kind of girl had been able to slow down my brother long enough for serious dating. He was always "on the go" and terribly popular. When he was in high school, there were often enough of his friends to have two basketball teams playing on the court on our back lawn. Guys were drawn to John because he was easygoing and dependable, and he loved sports. I could hardly believe that he was actually ready for a steady girlfriend. Yet he was bringing home someone that he wanted the family to meet. That sounded rather serious, so I looked forward to meeting her; but I was not prepared for the occasion.

When my younger brother Jim, a robust, curly-haired sportsman, came in from grade school, he was accompanied by several friends. They were planning a short swim in our pool; but Mother went out and told them that a special event was taking place that afternoon, and she would rather they swim the next day. Jim was not happy with the situation, but his friends agreed immediately and left.

"Jim," Mother called when he started up the stairs to his room. "Just a minute! I'm sorry about the swim, but you forgot that John is bringing his girlfriend home today. We want to make a very good impression."

"Well, I could wave at her from the pool."

Mother laughed. "You know better. We want to show the young lady what a fine family we are."

Jim made a face and started up the stairs.

Mother called after him. "Put on a clean shirt and a tie, please!"

"Aw, Mother," he yelled back, but as he ran on, he said he would do as she wished.

She turned toward me and added, "That goes for you too, darling."

I smiled. "Well, you certainly want to impress this newcomer."

Mother put her hands together as she usually did when wanting to discuss something. "Tom, you've got to help me. Remember. John needs our support."

"Sure, Mother," I replied and continued stacking logs. "For your sake, I hope it all goes very well."

"Thank you darling," she said, most pleased. Yet it was still evident that she was a bit nervous about the upcoming meeting. I was amused that she would be so uptight about something so ordinary. I supposed that she wanted to keep the status quo—a very content family. How proud she was when she walked into our church with her husband and three sons trailing behind her. The respect we had in our community meant a lot to her, and she did not want it disturbed. We were considered by neighbors and townspeople to be a very upstanding and happy family.

Father, an artist who had a rather large clientele, returned from his gallery just as I got the fire going. "Mother must be expecting a blizzard this evening," he commented in his soft, joking manner. "Of course, she likes a fire on a cool spring evening." I nodded as he passed by and started into the hall where the stairs were located.

"Yes," I called to him, "and she wants us in clean shirts and ties."

Father did not answer, which was his usual custom when an answer wasn't needed. He was a quiet, little man and very talented. He loved peace and quiet, a quality that was to make him an easy victim of the monster that was soon to make an appearance. Since Mother had inherited a farm that provided our family's upscale status, Father had always been submissive. We boys never went to him for money; we soon learned in turn that Mother was the source. Her religion was based on helping others, and that included her sons.

The family was seated around the fireplace when my brother John drove past a picture window with his beloved. The time for the big event had come. Mother was the first to rise and go out onto the patio. We all waited as John escorted the newcomer from the garage and down the walk toward the house. The rest of the family joined Mother, and we waited patiently. We were eager to meet the girlfriend and happy for John. How could we have envisioned the misery we would soon be experiencing? How naïve we were in our bastion of love and companionship! How unprepared we were! We had never met such a challenge, and that was the cause of our downfall. We were simply innocent children waiting to be slaughtered.

Suddenly, in the early evening shadows, I saw the long-awaited guest's face. I was stupefied. "She's gorgeous," I whispered as they came closer.

"Yes, she is," Mother whispered and left the patio followed by Slep. Walking toward the couple, Mother opened her arms for an embrace, but Slep stopped and sheepishly backed up a few steps Then he walked off into the grass. Such behavior was very unusual for him, because he usually greeted guests most warmly.

Suddenly I noticed that Mother had also stopped abruptly. Her arms fell slowly to her side. When she was in front of her son and his girlfriend, I heard a voice so sweet, one would have thought it was from heaven. "How do you do, Mrs. Whitney." The young woman extended a hand to my Mother, who was engrossed by the lovely smile before her. After a second of reckoning, she raised an arm to shake hands with the lady in front of her.

"Mother, I want you to meet Rosemary. Is she not beautiful?" my brother said, but his voice sounded completely different from anything I had heard in my life. The joyousness so plentiful in our mutual communications was missing.

"She certainly is," Mother commented. "And I—"

At that point, Mother was interrupted by the newcomer. "Mrs. Whitney, you need not agree with him. Let us remember that our Lord Jesus did not approve of flattery."

And so it began. Her words were like a savage wind suddenly blowing through the peaceful evening. She was already in charge; and Jesus, unbeknownst to His Majesty, was her helper. We were a Christian family, and we often attended a church on Sundays, but we would never embarrass someone as she had done. Her comment about flattery was rude. Mother turned and started back to the patio. It was obvious by the expression on her face that she was troubled. When the three of them reached us, Mother opened her mouth for introductions, but Rosemary intervened and said in the sweetest of tones, "Now, you must be Father Whitney."

Before my father could affirm his identification, she cast her large eyes at me. I immediately felt as if I was being induced into some kind of hypnotic trance. There was something in her eyes that gave the impression that she was looking straight into your soul. I did answer, "Yes, I'm Tom," but she only smiled sweetly and placed her hand on Jim's head. He had been standing by me, but when she touched him, he jumped back. "Oh, how sweet!" Rosemary sighed, and it almost seemed as if what she had done had been very kind and appropriate. Our family was absolutely taken aback by the newcomer, and we behaved as we had never done before. We were silent. It was Rosemary, of course, who continued. "What a wonderful family you have, John."

John could sense the reaction that had transpired and sort of stuttered when he said, "Why don't we all go into the family room. I see a fire in the fireplace."

"Oh, how charming," Rosemary exclaimed, adjusting a hand-knitted wrap around her shoulders. "There's nothing like a fire to take the chill off on a lovely spring evening." She sounded so pleasant, the family relaxed for a few moments. Then it was time for another bombshell.

Once inside the family room, I suggested a drink before dinner. "Oh, perhaps John would like to show me around a bit while you do that," Rosemary softly commented. Then she again set all of our nerves on edge. "You see, I don't drink. It's not a part of the Jesus Plan, you know."

Mother gave me a look that showed fearful concern, and Father withheld a smile. John's forehead wrinkled in disapproval, but Rosemary conquered all. As if she hadn't even heard me, she said, "John, shall we have a walk around?"

He quickly took her arm and led her to the patio and then out into the twilight on the lawn.

The family stood dumbstruck. When the couple was out of sight, Jim said, "I don't like her. She gives me the creeps!"

"It's those eyes," I said. "She could bore a hole through granite with them."

Mother protested. "Now, we must be kind. Remember, it's John's girlfriend, and she could be our new daughter-in-law. And, Tom, you promised you would not argue with her over religion."

"Mother, I only offered a drink."

Father commented, "It seems that she has her own set of rules."

Mother again defended the fiend. "It's too early for such generalizations. She's very sweet and caring most of the time."

I asked, "What's that 'Jesus Plan' she's talking about?"

Mother answered, "Oh, it surely means that we must live as Christ would want us to. That's the way you were brought up. She's just a bit more serious than we are."

"Not very cool, I'd say," Jim blurted out. He started out of the room.

Mother scolded him but raised her voice for all to hear. "We must remember that our dear John is involved. We cannot lose him. If he marries her, we must make the best of it. I want that understood."

Everyone agreed.

When it was time for the evening meal in the dining room, I had the privilege of calling the happy couple. John seated the newcomer next to him across from Jim and me. Whenever my eyes met Rosemary's, she would give a most ingratiating smile. I could only think of a big sack of sugar sitting there.

When Mother sat down at her place at one end of the table, Father, at the other end, picked up a knife to cut the roast beef in front of him. Jim picked up a bowl of potatoes.

"Don't you say grace?" Rosemary asked nonchalantly.

Everyone froze. Mother finally said, "We don't always, but we would be glad to this evening."

A kind smile crossed Rosemary's face. "It's the Jesus Plan, you know."

Mother nodded and said, "Would you like to say grace for us?"

Rosemary nodded, put her hands on her lap and closed her eyes. I supposed that Jesus didn't want anyone peeking. Then it happened. If a dragon had let loose a spray of fire down that table, I would not have been more surprised. She raised her head heavenward, keeping her eyes closed.

In a soft tone that only an angel would use on special occasions, Rosemary began. "Lord Jesus, help this family to see Thy Holy Light." After a slight pause, she continued, "And bless this food that we shall partake of. In Thy holy name, Amen."

No one knew what to do. There was an awkward silence until Mother said, "Thank you, Rosemary. That was most inspiring."

Rosemary's face reflected a smile of such contentment you would have thought that she had pulled us all out of a sinking boat. I realized then that I actually loathed her.

Father again lifted the carving knife, and we all passed various dishes to the right. It was the quietest dinner ever had by the Whitney family. Mother pulled us through the long, drawn-out affair by asking, in a delicate manner, questions about Rosemary's background.

"I must confess, Rosemary, that our John has surprised us with your visit, and we're most happy about it."

The guest glanced around the table with a condescending smile. Then she turned to John. "Why didn't you tell them earlier?"

"Forgive me, my dear," John said softly, "but remember, you weren't quite sure that you could come. There was that church meeting you thought you had to attend."

"Oh, John," she gushed, "you know I wouldn't let that stand in the way of meeting your wonderful family."

"Thank you, dear," Mother commented and asked, "Where does your family live?"

"Oh, John," Rosemary gasped, "You haven't told them anything. Well, let me fill you in. My parents are practically neighbors. They live in Evanston."

"Why, how wonderful," Mother responded. "If we had known, we could have invited them here for the evening."

Shaking a finger at my brother, Rosemary said, "Aren't you ashamed, you naughty boy? My folks would have loved to come."

So the banter went on and on. It amounted to worse news than we could have expected. Rosemary was from a very religious family. There was no surprise there, of course. Her father, Mr. Samuel Shane, was a minister in a protestant church named—I could have guessed—"The Jesus Plan." There was no escaping that plan. Everything led back to it. By the time the dinner was over, I was ready for excommunication or a hanging on a cross. The Whitney family was being invaded, and the invader was winning. I didn't know what to do.

That evening when John and Rosemary had left, the family gathered in the family room, which had been enlarged some time back by enclosing a side patio. A leather couch and lounge chairs faced the fireplace where my parents had chairs on each side. In the back of the room was a large niche where we kept our computer. After we had settled down, our discussion began with a few unimportant matters; but it seemed that everyone was anxious to talk about the impression that Rosemary had made on each of us. Jim had already expressed his view and had been bawled out. I felt that I should lead the charge. "Mother and Dad, I have to say it. That woman was not kind, even though she wanted to give that impression."

Holding her hands together and shaking her head slightly, Mother said, "Isn't it really too early for us to be so judgmental?"

Father, always the peacemaker, said, "She was probably just a bit nervous. After all, it was her first time here."

I could not stand their efforts at accommodation and said, "She's a cold duck if ever I met one. What on earth does John see in her?"

No one could answer, and we sat silently until Jim stood and ran toward a door saying, "I've got to call a friend. Is that allowed in the Jesus Plan?"

Mother raised her voice and called, "Jim!" but it was too late. He was out of the room.

Father commented, "She did sort of run that into the ground."

"Goodness!" Mother exclaimed. "What is happening to us? I was so thrilled that John had found someone, and now things seem so up in the air."

It was obvious that the whole family was upset, so I stayed by the fire when my parents retired. I wanted to talk with my brother when he returned after taking her home. I walked over to my computer in a far niche of the room and Googled "Jesus." I read very interesting information in a section about the life of the Lord. "There is no historical evidence that Jesus even existed." *Well, he sure does here!* I thought. "The biblical Gospels were written forty to sixty years apart." *No wonder there's such inconsistency about the life of Jesus!*

I continued reading until I saw the headlights of John's car. I was surprised. *Guess the Jesus Plan puts one to bed early and doesn't even allow a goodnight kiss.* When John walked into the room, I said, "Well, you've got something there!"

Misinterpreting what I meant, he smiled and said, "Isn't she something?"

"She sure is!" I sarcastically replied.

The look on John's face showed me that he had not understood my impression of Rosemary, and it was obvious that I had said the wrong thing. "What's wrong with her?" he asked.

"Well, she just about Jesus-Planned me to death!" I replied. "She even—"

John interrupted. "Oh, you just didn't understand her. She was merely trying to help you. You see, she has Jesus in her heart, and she wants to share Him with others."

I looked at my brother and thought, *Did he really say that? He had never been overly religious before, and now he sounded just like her.* "John!" I exclaimed, "What has come over you? Believing in Jesus is one thing, but to use him as a basis for being rude is quite another."

"What do you mean? She can't be rude. She's so kind and sweet. How was she rude?"

I again looked at my brother in amazement. It was obvious that he was under the spell or influence of that *fiend*, an appellation that I used for the first time in my mind. "John, you're kidding. What about her insisting on prayer at dinner?"

"Well, she was used to it and thought she should ask."

"You don't think it was rude to force us into a prayer?"

"How could a prayer be rude?"

My hands went up in the air. "Gosh, John, if you can't see through that woman, then you really are lost."

Again his look showed his confusion. We were not communicating. There was no common ground between us. Suddenly it seemed that neither of us had anything to say. John rose and said as he left the room, "We'll talk about it tomorrow."

I nodded, but for the first time in my life, I felt as if I had lost my brother.

Our conversation did not resume the next day as planned. John left early in the morning so he could join Rosemary at her father's church. The girlfriend wanted her beau with her, according to the Jesus Plan, which evidently demanded togetherness similar to being tied with rope. My brother began spending more and more time with the Shane family. Our parents assumed that he was also investigating possible positions of employment. Since that subject was never mentioned during John's occasional short talks with the family, Mother finally asked, "Have you thought of what you might want to do, now that you seem to be thinking of settling down?"

"Of course, Mother," he responded. "In fact, at the church, Reverend Shane has introduced me to several members of his congregation who seem interested in having me work for them."

"How splendid!" she exclaimed. "And what sort of work would that be?" she asked, knowing that our entire family was curious.

"Oh, a Mr. Boxter wants me in his warehouse as a supervisor. Of course, I'd have to work my way up to that position."

A frown spread over our mother's face. "Oh, John, you surely wouldn't be happy in some sort of warehouse position. Would you?"

John seemed surprised at her question. "Why not?"

"What about college?" I asked. "You've got the GI Bill now."

"Oh, Rosemary doesn't think I should bother with higher education. You know, it's considered best now to just get into the work force."

Perplexed, Mother continued in a sorrowful tone, "John, you know that we've always dreamed of all of our sons going to college."

John frowned and looked at the floor. "I know, but Rosemary feels that college just isn't part of the Jesus Plan."

I laughed, but Mother cast a menacing glance at me. "John, surely you don't assume that the church has anything to do with your education? You must prepare for the problems ahead. When you marry, there will be so many financial matters and adjustments."

In an earnest tone, John continued, "But that's what I'm considering. Rosemary feels that we would be much happier if we just stayed as we are, safe in the Jesus Plan."

Father finally joined in. "In such a situation, what is the Jesus Plan?"

"It's wonderful, Dad," John replied with enthusiasm. "Everything is planned out for you. You just put yourself in the hands of Jesus."

"Sounds to me," I interjected, "like you're in the hands of Rosemary!"

John snapped at me. "A college punk like you wouldn't understand."

"Boys!" Mother exclaimed. "This is a serious matter, and John is explaining his side. We need to understand before we can comment." She looked at me again, showing her disappointment.

John continued, "What's wrong with managing a warehouse?"

There was a brief silence. Finally Mother said, "John, all your life you've known that we wanted a college education for our sons. Remember when you joined the army and we tried changing your mind? We thought you should continue your college education and then go into the service if you wished."

"We've been through all of that," John insisted. "There's no need to repeat it. Besides, I know that Rosemary is right. We'll be very happy living a proper life in the Jesus Plan."

After a brief silence, Father asked, "You've not been very clear about what you are calling the Jesus Plan. We have always been Christians. How is your church different?"

Mother and I exchanged glances. John noticed our behavior and said, "I have the impression that you are against me. That you don't want me to marry Rosemary."

"John, my dear boy," Mother exclaimed. "You're wrong. We have nothing against Rosemary. We just want to understand why there is such a change in you."

My brother turned his head slightly askance. He looked almost in pain. "I've not changed, Mother. I just feel now that I've sort of found myself, that I have a purpose in life. You know how I've been neither here nor there most of the time. I've tried this and that, but now I have something I feel I can really succeed in."

"What's that?" I asked, adding, "and don't tell me it's the Jesus Plan."

John frowned and shook his head. Gazing at me rather severely, he said, "You'd never understand. You take everything for granted. It's all a straight path for you."

"What do you mean?" I asked.

Mother interrupted. "Boys, don't turn on each other. You're brothers, and you both care deeply about each other."

Father asked, "Are you thinking of the ministry?"

John laughed. "Oh, no, Dad. I just want to continue my feeling of security. I've never felt so sure about anything in my life. You see, in the Jesus Plan, my path is laid out for me. Rosemary has convinced me that I have found what I've been seeking."

"But you've always been a Christian," Father stated.

"Dad," John responded, "our church has never given me any direction, but I have found it in the Jesus Plan."

"Which is?" I asked.

Turning to me, he replied, "A way of life that will have direction and meaning. I understand now that I can make a contribution to the welfare of humanity, and I know that will bring me happiness. Rosemary has convinced me of that."

We were silent. Everything always reverted to Rosemary. Mother changed the subject, saying, "If you've found happiness, my dear boy, then everything is fine."

Father agreed and avoided an argument, but he did make a suggestion that seemed out of character. He usually left invitations to our home in our mother's realm of activity. Yet he said, leaning toward his wife, "My dear, I think we should invite the Shanes for dinner. Shouldn't our families know each other?"

Mother nodded and said to John, "Please invite your friends for dinner. We would love to meet them."

John seemed very pleased with the idea, but I thought, *I wonder what kind of monsters they are?* We were soon to find out.

The occasion for meeting the Shanes was set up for the next weekend, and it had more in store for us than we could possibly have imagined. First, we were to attend their Sunday morning church service, and then they would come to our home for dinner. It appeared to be the perfect way for the families to get to know each other.

Our family arrived at the small, wooden Church of the Jesus Plan on time to be welcomed at the entranceway by Reverend Shane, whose severe visage had a threatening aspect. I was sure that Slep would have barked at him had he been with us. It was obvious from whom Rosemary had inherited her large, dark, piercing eyes. The Reverend gleamed down at us as if he were conducting an inspection. When Mother and Dad were in front of him, he raised a hand and made a sign of the cross over each of them. I say "a" sign because it was neither Catholic nor Eastern Orthodox; it was probably his own invention. It was as if he drew a straight line in front of one's face and then crossed it. My father had raised his hand for a shake but slowly lowered it as he watched the man give his blessing. When the Reverend finished, he said in a deep, unpleasantly raspy voice, "My blessed wife is at the organ and will greet you after our service." My father thanked him. In the meantime my brother Jim and I had been able to walk behind our parents without receiving an introduction. Then our family entered the austere chapel, passing several rows of seats before sitting down near the organ.

Mrs. Gertrude Shane, who had been informed of our arrival, turned and gave us a nod while her lips whispered, *Welcome!* She had a ruddy complexion and was so short she had trouble reaching the organ's pedals. However, her size did not hinder her enthusiasm in squirming around on the organ bench so that she could fill the small hall with loud huffs and puffs from the inner workings of the old instrument. She also sang in a high shrill voice.

Jim snickered, but Mother quickly gave him a look of disapproval. The songs with which Gertrude filled the hall were unknown to us. This seemed unusual since we too were Protestant. The Jesus Plan had even changed the old familiar clamor. There was nothing we could do but wait patiently until the service started. Reverend Harry Shane was a tall, thin, wrinkled man who had never graduated from a Christian college. He used the oldest joke in the category of corny taste: "I decided that PC meant for me to preach Christ rather than plant corn." It was a Sunday I shall never repeat.

When my brother John, dressed in a three-button black jacket, escorted his girlfriend past our row of seats, he turned to us with a smile that showed his gratitude for our being there. The vampire, expressing her purity by wearing a white dress with a long, white silk scarf, also looked down at us, but her expression showed heartwarming condescension. She had brought us all into the Jesus Plan, and her imagined triumph was evident in her constrained haughtiness. Jim stuck his tongue out after they had passed, but Mother quickly tapped his knee and whispered, "Behave!"

The small hall filled with people, and when Reverend Shane took a seat on the small stage at the front of the building, the crowd stood up and burst into a joyful song led, of course, by Gertrude. The five verses of "Jesus Save Us" seemed interminable, but their message was clear. It was Jesus all the way! This was especially emphasized in the Reverend's prattle, which droned on for three quarters of an hour. If such a talk had been given at my college, I and everyone else would have walked out.

The sermon was almost incoherent. It was filled with hypotheses without any factual basis, repetitions of biblical quotations without any understandable association, and continual conclusions without any proven criteria. The service was a monstrous example of the hypocrisy and ignorance that I had read about in so many cults and off-shoots of the Christian faith. I was appalled that my brother had been taken in by such irrationality.

When the Reverend finally ended his parochial discourse, several of the Chosen—that is, those who had fulfilled the Jesus Plan—passed out trays containing tiny communion cups filled with grape juice. When I took one and passed the tray on to the others, I raised the so-called wine to my lips and thought: *Here's to Jesus!* Perhaps that was a bit irreligious, but I was fed up with the whole scene. I wished that I could express myself by shouting something profane; but I wouldn't have been heard, even if I had cried out, because Gertrude was filling the hall with moans from the organ.

Just as communion was about finished, the Chosen were back with their trays for the giving of one's weekly tithe. Needless to say, I did not contribute money for the support of a church based on ignorance, but my father did so out of politeness. When we were leaving the church, Mother whispered to me, "Tom, darling, don't say anything disrespectful to him." I nodded my assurance and walked beside her as we approached the minister. He bowed to us but did not smile. Instead his face reflected a sort of supercilious satisfaction. He was in a state of ecstasy over having once again carried out his great mission of spreading the gospel—and spreading it very thin, in my opinion. Yet His Holiness did nod when my father reminded him that we were expecting his family at our dinner table.

Driving home, the family was silent until Jim began expressing his view of the church service. He was disgusted. He could not understand what the minister was talking about, and he thought the music was cacophonous. He was correct of course, and Father surprised me by agreeing. Yet, before Mother could start her usual rebuttal, I managed to express my opinion.

"Listen, we've got a real problem. That church is dangerous. Its literal interpretation of the Bible is absurd, and it's making its flock of followers into hypocritical Nazis. Reverend Shane is pompous and ignorant. He preaches prejudice more than moral values. When he said that a divorced man cannot expect a heavenly reward, he was generalizing without criteria. I think he just babbles anything he wants. How John can accept such drivel is beyond me. We've got to stop that wedding."

"Tom," Mother finally interjected, "we've no right to condemn people who are honestly and sincerely expressing their faith. While we see Jesus differently from the way they do, it doesn't mean that they are wrong, does it? Besides, we shouldn't judge so severely after hearing only one sermon. Should we?"

I laughed and responded. "And why shouldn't we? If I had to sit through another talk like that, I'd never go to church again."

"Tom," Mother repeated, trying to calm me down. "We've got to think of John. If he brings Rosemary into our family and attends her church, we have got to find understanding. It's true that they do not interpret the Scriptures as we do, but—I'll say it again—that doesn't mean they are wrong. It's too early to criticize."

Jim said, "But he didn't make sense!"

"We've got to think of John!" Mother insisted.

"Well, I can have my own opinion," Jim said and sat back on the car seat.

Exasperated, Mother stated, "My dears, I ask only one thing now. When the Shanes are with us as guests, please do not argue with the Reverend. Do it for John's sake, please!"

Everyone agreed. We would behave at the table . . . somewhat.

When we turned into our driveway, Father said, "It will be difficult to keep a straight face."

I laughed and said, "I'll say."

"What'll we do if she sings?" Jim asked. He laughed and made a high-pitched noise.

"Oh, boys," Mother appealed in a downcast voice, "please behave. We must help John."

The rest of us uttered various replies as we departed the car, but we finally assured Mother that we would be on our best behavior.

Inside the house, I went to my computer and looked at my e-mails. My parents came into the family room and sat down by the fireplace. When they started talking, I realized that they had not noticed me back in the niche. Mother said, "I'm worried about Tom too. He seems to be so irreligious anymore. Is that what they teach in college these days?"

Father answered, "Well, we did name him 'doubting Thomas.'"

"I'm not joking," Mother responded. "We brought them up in a church, and they never caused any trouble. Well, a few times Tom asked questions he should not have . . . like that time in Sunday school when he asked if Jesus played with himself."

Father laughed. "I liked the time when someone asked him why the whale swallowed Jonah, and he answered, 'Because he was hungry.'"

"Yes, he could be naughty, but for the most part, it seems that his faith is secure . . . that he believes as we do."

"Tom's lost in the world of ideas. He's meeting challenges at school that are causing him to think. I believe he's fine. Let him philosophize if he wishes. It's better than acting as if Christ is the man next door—like John does these days."

Mother shook her head. "Well, I just hope he behaves when the Shanes arrive. I don't want to embarrass John."

"He will," Father assured her.

The Shanes were very late. Our family was used to eating after arriving home from church. Mother always left a pot roast baking in the oven, and we would have dinner immediately so that everyone could do whatever activity they wanted in the afternoon. As we became increasingly hungry while waiting for the Shanes, Jim and I would slip into the kitchen and snitch a piece of celery or a carrot stick. By three o'clock, Mother became worried. She mulled over our presence at the church but could not think of anything we'd done that might have offended the Shanes. Jim commented, "Oh, I hope we did!"

His remark did not please Mother, but she finally concluded that the Shanes were late merely because members of their congregation probably talked with them after the service. "After all," she said, "the Reverend is their pastor, and they depend on him for guidance."

"He'd lead me to hell," I quickly said, and Jim laughed.

Mother again raised her voice. "Boys, you promised to behave."

"I was just joking, Mother. We'll be good."

Satisfied, Mother placed her roast back in the oven to keep it warm. At three thirty, Jim ran into the kitchen and yelled, "They're coming up the drive!"

The moment had arrived. I was sure that each member of the family was experiencing some agitation—perhaps even fear. We were up against a situation that was new to us. Never before had we felt threatened in this way, as if maybe we were not up to what was expected. We considered ourselves a normal, upscale family, and if we thought someone did not care for us, it was their problem. We were amiable people and had nothing to prove to anyone. With the Shanes, however, it was different. We wanted to be approved for John's sake, and we were not sure we knew how to do it.

I noticed our nervousness in the way we had changed seats in the family room. For some reason, Mother did not sit in her comfortable chair by the fireplace. She sat down on the couch in front of the mantel. Jim ran in with Slep and walked over to a window where he could observe the approach of the guests. Father remained standing for a while, but sat down on a bench near the door when Jim said that the Shanes were coming up the walk. I had taken a seat by a reading table but stood up when the others did. We heard the door to the sunroom open. Not one of us said a word, and we stood in our awkward positions as if we were statues.

John entered first, leading Rosemary by the arm. Slep quickly ran past them into the entrance hall. John called after the dog, but he did not return. Rosemary smiled and said, "Dogs just don't like me." Then she put out a hand to Mother who had come up to greet her. "And how are you, Mother, dear?" Rosemary asked.

Before she could answer, Samuel and Gertrude entered. Smiling, Mother went to Mrs. Shane and held out her hand. They shook hands. Father did the same with the Reverend. Someone suggested that we sit down. I cannot remember who said it, but it was at that moment that our torment started. Mr. Samuel Shane suddenly rendered a throaty appeal: "May I bless this house at this time?"

Mother and Father both agreed that he could and stepped back from the Shanes as Gertrude began a shrill paean, "Follow us, Jesus!" I looked at Jim, and he slipped out of the room. His quick action went unnoticed by our guests, who appeared to be involved in the delivery of one of their favorite hymns of praise. When the high, raspy notes finished, the Reverend delivered his message in a loud, sanctimonious voice. "Lord Jesus, bless this house that is so in need. Amen!"

Rosemary repeated the "Amen" and nudged John, who then repeated it as well. Mother and Father seemed paralyzed but quickly regained their composure. The Shanes walked over by the fireplace and surveyed the room as if they were making an inspection. Rosemary, with a smile so sweet it was sickening, led me over to the minister for a blessing. Before I could say anything that might be disturbing, Mother announced, "Instead of sitting down now, I suggest we go into the dining room first and have our dinner. John, will you please show the Shanes the way while I go to the kitchen?" He agreed and walked ahead so that they could follow.

Seating at the dining room table was arranged by Rosemary. By then, Jim had slipped back into the room, and she placed him with the Reverend and Gertrude on one side of the table, while I sat with John and his girlfriend on the other. After Mother brought in the roast beef and placed it on a serving cart by her side, she asked the minister if he would like to say grace. He gladly accepted and took a ceremonious pose, placing his elbows on the table, folding his hands together, and raising his head skyward. His upward stare was so severe that one could not help but look at the ceiling. Then he started a sermon, not a prayer. I was sure Mother would have liked to place the roast back in the oven. When he finally finished, Mother began passing dishes to the customary right. Mr. Shane helped himself to the beef and then handed the platter across the table to me. I wanted to say, "Pass it to the right," but caught myself in time and took the dish. Soon dishes were being passed in all directions—across the table and to the right and left. It was a muddle, and Jim and I almost laughed.

When the food was distributed, the Reverend suggested that we give thanks for the nourishment God had provided. Mother had to agree. Again the holy man thanked God for the "vitals," as he put it, before us. Finally we began eating. A sudden quietness at the table was evident. No one knew how to start the conversation, so we ate. Finally Mother stated, "Reverend Shane, we want to thank you for your fine sermon this morning."

"Sister Whitney," His Eminence replied to my mother, "I was thankful that our daughter invited you."

Rosemary also thanked Mother for mentioning the inspiring sermon and then made a strange comment. "Your words make me realize that you are capable of achieving the Jesus Plan."

Mother smiled, but did not answer. I could have said plenty, but I held my tongue.

Brother John changed the subject with a bombshell. "Mother and Dad and Reverend and Mrs. Shane, I have wonderful news." He looked to the side at Rosemary, and they both smiled. Her large eyes had a twinkle that somehow suggested, *You're doing what I told you to!* "Rosemary and I are engaged!"

Mrs. Shane clapped her hands together and shouted, "Halleluiah!"

For a few seconds there was complete silence. We were to be sorry about that quietness much later, but at the time, everyone was too taken aback to speak. Finally mother said, "Oh, John, you have surprised us!"

Reverend Shane immediately began blessing the couple. The rest of us just sat in shock and allowed our dinner to become cold. While he was mouthing off all sorts of biblical quotations and plenty of mumbo jumbo, Rosemary twisted around a ring on her third finger and revealed a fairly large diamond. They were engaged!

We all made our compliments, of course, but most of them did not seem heartfelt. I could hardly utter my congratulations. I simply could not believe that my brother would still want to live with that woman after hearing her father's sermon. Had she so completely subdued him that he could not think? What was the attraction? I was dumbfounded, because it was the first time I knew for sure that she had some kind of power over him.

When a lull finally came in the conversation, I decided on action. I asked the Reverend if the "beast" he had talked about in his sermon came from the book of Revelation.

"Most certainly," His Eminence decreed. "That is one of the greatest books in the Bible."

"That is interesting," I commented. "I've always wondered why Revelation was chosen to be in the great book when there were so many other revelations written at that time."

The minister seemed to stiffen. He sat back on his chair, rigid and straight, so I continued. "You know that revelations were a popular literary genre in the third century AD."

It was obvious from the expression on the Reverend's face that he did not know. In fact, it appeared that he did not know the word "genre" either.

Mr. Shane's visage turned to bewilderment. He was cornered and knew it, so he looked at his daughter for help.

Rosemary immediately came to his rescue. Turning toward me, she kindly said, "You probably did not understand the message that my father was giving in his sermon."

"Oh? And what was that?" I replied.

"What he said about the beast."

"What about the beast?"

"That it is among us at all times."

The Reverend had regained his composure and almost shouted, "Yes, that is it. The beast is among us at all times."

"Which beast?" I asked, having fortunately remembered from Bible classes at our church that John, the writer of Revelation, had mentioned several types of beasts. They had stuck in my memory because a friend and I had made much fun of them when the instructor tried explaining them.

Rosemary tried a rebuttal. "What do you mean, *which beast?*"

"Well, as I remember, there was one with ten heads and another with two horns."

"Preposterous!" she exclaimed.

I was delighted with her answer, because it showed that she did not know either.

"No, he's right," the Reverend admitted and looked downcast.

At this point, Mother interrupted. "Well, I think we've talked enough about something so horrible. Let's retire to the family room for dessert and coffee."

The Shanes were quite agreeable, but Rosemary was silent. She could not be embarrassed or beaten. I did not know the depth of her evil at that time, but she was already planning her revenge.

The group retired to the family room where my father tried discussing modern art with Mr. Shane. The latter was only interested in religious art and considered anything else a waste of time and almost sinful. Mother then tried carrying the conversation by asking Mrs. Shane if she liked the sweet potato and cranberry dish that had been served at dinner. The latter did not know that there were cranberries in the dish, but she had wondered what gave the potatoes such a peculiar taste. Since both Mother and Father had failed to find a worthy topic of conversation, I decided that I should help them find a common thread that would be of interest to our guests. Mother did have a rather fearful look when I started talking, but I had already introduced a religious theme before she could stop me. I asked the Reverend if he enjoyed reading about the history of the Bible. That simple question brought on a tirade. Again in his sonorous voice he said, "The gospel was given to us by God Almighty. One should read the Bible rather than theories about its creation."

I was delighted with his outburst, for I knew I had discovered another subject that he knew very little about. So I lied. "I rather enjoy reading about the creation of the famous book."

Jim asked, "Wasn't it written all at once?"

Avoiding Jim's question and bristling, the Reverend responded quickly and angrily, "When God creates, it is perfect, and so is the Bible."

"Well, as I remember, at the Council of Nicaea, there was a great deal of argument about just which chapters should be put into the book."

The minister just sat and stared at me. I almost laughed.

Rosemary again came to his aid. Looking rather severely at me, she said, "I doubt that you've ever read anything about the Council of Nicaea. Besides, my father has already dismissed that subject as uneventful and not useful."

My brother John added, "I'm sure Tom hasn't read anything about it."

In my own defense, I gave a rebuttal. "I remember that, in Miss Woden's Sunday school class, we talked about that council that took place in the fifth century BC."

"Boys!" Mother called out and laughed. "What a thing to be talking about. Let's discuss the good news that John and Rosemary have given us."

I withdrew, satisfied that I had won the debate. If the Reverend had known anything about that famous council, he would have corrected me with great pleasure. The council was not in the fifth century BC. I had tricked him, and he didn't know it. I would have liked to embarrass him further, but I realized that I was tormenting Mother, so I said, "Yes, let's talk about the happy occasion."

Mother turned toward Rosemary and asked, "What plans have you two made?"

Rosemary smiled sweetly again. "Oh, we've just begun making plans. We'll be informing everyone about them later."

Mother took Rosemary's hand, but she abruptly pulled it away. A soft smile faded from Mother's face, but she kindly said, "Well, if there's anything that I can help you with, you know that I want to."

Gertrude broke in. "Oh, it won't be a large wedding. If we invited the church, the ceremony would take forever."

It will anyway! I thought.

Mother turned to Gertrude. "You will, I'm sure, allow me to invite our closest friends. Everyone will be so excited. You know that our John is greatly loved by his and our friends."

Gertrude sort of stiffened and nodded toward John and Rosemary. "We'll let the young ones decide."

"Well, I'm sure they'll want John's friends," Mother said.

Rosemary did not answer, but turned to her father. "It'll soon be time for the evening service, so I guess we should leave."

Evening service! I wanted to scream. *I'd rather die!*

John stood and asked the family if we would like to attend with them. Father, thank God, made an excuse, saying that he had some paint that he did not want dried out. Jim professed homework, and I didn't answer. Mother said, "I think we'll do that another time, if you don't mind."

The Reverend stood up and gave us all a blessing before saying, "One cannot hear the word of God too many times."

"I'm sure," Mother agreed.

"Yes," Gertrude added, "It's not wise to miss a service. It is part of the Jesus Plan, you know."

I only knew one thing: I'd flunk the Jesus Plan.

Mother and Dad escorted the departing guests to their car. John said he would be back after the service, and then opened a door for Rosemary. My parents watched and waved as they drove away.

Back in the family room, we held a family conference. I started the harangue. "What are we going to do?" I asked as we settled in our usual seats around the fireplace.

Jim spread out on the couch with Slep and quickly commented, "They make me sick. I can't stand 'em."

There was a brief silence during which Mother broke down. "My dears, it appears that John is planning to marry her, and we must accept her."

"But there's something strange about her," Jim said with a strained look on his face. "I can't stand her. I think she's got the Evil Eye."

"Jim!" Mother exclaimed. "Don't be morbid. We hardly know Rosemary. She's usually very sweet."

Jim sat up and looked at Slep so hard the dog raised its head. "Yeah, she's sweet until she looks through her Evil Eye!"

"Jim, that's enough!" Mother scolded.

"But I can't stand her!" he replied.

"My boys," Mother continued. "We will have to stand her and accept her into the family. We've got to think of John. We don't want to lose him. He left us once for the army, and now he's going off again."

"I'm afraid we have lost him already," Father stated. "I don't see how we can overcome the hold she has on him."

"Yeah," I agreed. "He seems determined to join the Jesus Plan, whatever it is, and I don't think he's doing it on his own. She's forcing him into it."

"Tom," Mother said, "that's a strong word. John surely has more willpower than that."

"I don't think so. She's caught him at just the right time. He can't decide on what he wants to do, and it seems that she's got the perfect plan for him."

"Why do you say that?" Father asked.

"The Jesus Plan evidently has an answer for everything, like in the Catholic Church. My friend Joe has a brother who became a priest. The family wasn't Catholic and was disturbed by their son's becoming a member, let alone a priest. When he was ordained, they asked him what his duties were. He had become a marriage counselor. Since he had never been married, they asked how he could answer the questions that would be asked. He said that he was given a large book that had answers for all the questions."

Father and I laughed.

Jim interjected, "So John just has to read from the Jesus Plan's big book!" He then yelled "Jesus" so loud that it scared Slep and made him jump off the couch.

"Jim, don't be so irreligious!" Mother warned. Then she asked, "Is there a book that explains the Jesus Plan?"

Father commented, "There doesn't seem to be. If there was, I'm sure the Reverend would have brought us one."

Jim said, "I hope it has pictures."

Mother shook her head. "Jim, you must be respectful."

"But Mother, I don't think I'd understand it without pictures."

I laughed.

Again there was silence until Mother said, "We just have to sit down with John and work this out. We can't lose him. There's got to be a way."

"He'll be home late," Jim commented.

Mother continued, "If he comes late, we can discuss it with him tomorrow. Whatever happens, we must hear his side of the story."

Chapter 2

The Meeting

At ten o'clock my parents and Jim retired, but I sat down at my computer and Googled the words "psychic vampire." To my surprise, I read in the section entitled "Vampires" that such a phenomenon is a being that feeds off the "life force" of other living creatures. *My God*, I thought, *that's Rosemary!* The article stated that such a person is represented in the occult beliefs of various cultures. *Heck! They're right here among us!* Yet it maintained that there is no medical proof that supports such a creature. *We've got proof!* I almost said it aloud. *She's here and she's sucking the life out of my brother!* I stared at the print, almost overwhelmed.

Then it came to me. She was using her religious ignorance to persuade John that he had been a sinner and she could save him! I was petrified for a few moments; then I read on. Suddenly I hesitated and looked at a picture above my computer. It was an image of Cossacks riding on fast horses. The artist, Vicki Doyle, had captured the wild nature of the beasts as they were rushing toward their objective. I gasped. Rosemary was like that, and she was fast closing in on the kill! How could I possibly stop her?

Suddenly I saw the light of John's car coming up the driveway, which interrupted my thoughts.

When he came in, I said, "John, I'd like to talk with you."

"And I with you," he responded rather roughly.

He sat down in Father's chair and faced me as I settled on the couch. Before I could speak, he angrily said, "How could you behave like you did? What did they do to you to make you act like you did?"

I smiled, but he snarled, "Don't laugh, it's not funny."

I straightened up and swung my legs off the couch. "No, it isn't funny," I said. "It's rather frightening."

"What do you mean?"

"It's hard for me to believe that you could be taken in by such people."

John stated frankly, "Be careful. I'm going to marry Rosemary."

I was silent for a few moments. I didn't want to upset him so much that he'd be irrational. So I started slowly. "John, we're brothers. You know that I only want the best for you."

"Well, you're not acting like it."

"John, maybe I feel that the Shanes aren't the best for you."

"Why?"

I sort of bit my lip, which was Mother's habit. "Well, first of all, Mr. Shane has got to be one of the most ignorant men I've ever met, and if you don't see it, we might as well stop talking."

John shook his head. "And since when did you, of all people, become an expert on the Bible?"

I almost laughed. "Well, we know that I'm not an expert on the Bible. I don't even remember having one in my hands. Yet if the Reverend Shane preaches the sort of stuff I've been hearing about the Jesus Plan, then I think I have the right to call him ignorant."

"How can you argue with someone who does know the Bible?"

"John, he doesn't know it. Surely you noticed that he was absolutely uninformed about the history of the Bible."

"He knows that God created it."

"Oh, yeah? Well, I know that several medieval councils had a lot to do with it. I got that in a history course I had in college."

"Colleges are famous for making atheists of students."

I smiled. "So you've been talking to the Reverend about me?"

"Yes, I have. Someone from our family had to apologize for the rude things you said to him."

"John!" I exclaimed. "Don't you see that I am trying to wake you up to what you're getting into?"

"And what am I getting into that's so bad?"

I shook my head. "Well, ignorance, for one thing! Reverend Shane is preaching a dangerous interpretation of the Bible. He doesn't really know what he's talking about. For instance, when he says so adamantly that a sinner will burn in hell, he doesn't realize that it's only an interpretation by a human being, not Christ. Dante even said that hell was icy cold. I got that in a literature course."

"Oh, just because you don't understand him, you criticize him."

Again I shook my head. "I'm also referring to Rosemary. I feel like she's duped you. You'd believe anything she says."

John's hands flew up into the air as if he did not know how to respond. "Tom," he finally said, "if you could only realize how thankful I am for what she's doing for me. I see things more clearly now than ever before. I know what I want, and I know what to do about it."

"Well, if she's given you such direction, what does she say you should do?"

"That's easy. Christ will direct me. He's showing me the way. If I have a question, I ask the Lord for help. He sends me a sign. I follow his advice. Why, just yesterday I needed to know whether I should change banks or not, so Rosemary suggested I rely on Christ's judgment. I prayed . . . and you know what happened? My billfold fell off my dresser, so I changed my bank."

I could hardly keep from laughing. "Listen, John. Christ is not the man next door. Rosemary is the one who is directing you right into her eternal grasp. She's thinking for you by having you ask the Lord for everything. Wake up!"

John shook his head. "Don't you believe in Christ anymore?"

I sort of stretched my lips. "John, belief in Christ is not the question. Our world is changing. Modern technology like the TV and the computer have awakened a global understanding. Globalization is changing our world. Through modern technology, we know more about everything around the globe. We don't think only about ourselves. We are becoming citizens of the world, not just Americans. We understand that we are being affected greatly by the politics and finances of other countries. Don't you see it?"

"Yes, our world has changed, but how does that affect our religion?"

"We see things in a broader spectrum. Even our Christian faith, which has given us satisfaction for so many centuries, has been challenged."

John interrupted me. "It sure has, and we must fight the infidels to save Christianity. I didn't realize this until Rosemary helped me understand how our true faith is being attacked."

My face must have shown anguish. "John, that's what the ignorant say. All the great religions claim that they're right and everyone else is wrong. But today we see a much wider view of the human dilemma. Mankind is beginning to realize that there has got to be something bigger than our individual creeds."

"Bigger than God?" John asked in a strained, fearful voice. "Are you crazy?"

"You don't understand what I mean. Unless the great religions find mutability, this species is doomed. There will just be endless wars."

John was quiet. When he stood up, he said, "You've gone too far astray or something. You'd better talk with Rosemary about this. I'm going to bed."

"Tell her I want to talk with her."

Passing me on the way to the stairs, John nodded and uttered, "I will."

The thought of discussing religion with his fiancée was not pleasant, but I wondered if it might not be the way to cause a rupture in their relationship. I began searching in my mind for some means of approaching the possibility, but I soon fell asleep.

About three in the morning, I awakened on the family room couch and again began thinking about the forthcoming catastrophe for our family. History had shown that mixing reason and religion does not produce positive results. I thought of the Old Believers in seventeenth-century Russia who went to their deaths rather than accept the reforms of the priest Nikon. The reforms made sense to many people, but because the changes affected centuries-old beliefs, the ignorant refused to consider them. It was the same with my brother. I somehow had to make him understand that he was being duped by an ignoramus. Yet the means by which I could attack the vampire remained unclear. I went upstairs to my room. For some time, I rolled and tossed in bed before sleep finally overcame me.

John was gone the next morning when I went down for breakfast. Mother said that he had left early because Rosemary wanted him for something. "Yeah, a beheading, no doubt." Mother was busy turning the pancakes on her grill and simply shook her head, but I said, "Oh, Mother, it's true. What are we going to do?"

She placed a plate of pancakes before me and again slightly shook her head when she answered. "I don't know, but I am greatly distressed about it. He doesn't have a job, and he's got to go to college. I can hardly sleep just thinking about it."

"Me too," I responded as I poured maple syrup on my pancakes. "Right now I think we'd be wise to see them together as much as possible. I want to talk with her. If she's as loony as her father, we're bound to have disagreements. Maybe John could see that the Jesus Plan is not for him. It's worth a try."

"Do be careful," Mother implored as she gave me a cup of coffee. "We can't offend her. John would be so upset, and that would not help us at all."

I nodded and quickly ate my pancakes. When I started out of the kitchen, Mother stopped me and said, "I'll invite them for lunch. Then you can talk with her."

Turning toward her, I smiled. "Yes, do that. Let's start our own Jesus Plan."

Mother could not help but laugh. "Now, Tom, don't tease. I don't think she can take it."

"I'm sure she wouldn't. She's serious stuff, and that's the problem. Our family's never been uptight, and that's why John's being taken in. She's stronger than he is, so she's able to subjugate him. What a life he'd have with her. He'd be her slave!"

Mother looked out the window of the kitchen nook briefly, then said, "Well, then, I'll invite them for lunch." She went to the phone and dialed the number John had written on a pad.

Mother hesitated when someone answered the phone. She asked, "John, is that you?" She put her hand over the receiver and whispered to me, "I think it's John, and he said, 'Jesus Plan! How can I help you?'" Her face showed her confusion, but she continued. "John, dear, I would like for you and Rosemary to come for lunch today. Can you?" She listened and then said, "Oh, I'm sorry, but we'll be glad to see you."

I knew that Rosemary was not coming, but perhaps it was best. When she hung up the phone, she had tears in her eyes. I went to her and put my arm around her. "Oh, it's much more serious than we thought. Now he's working for them."

Neither of us wanted conversation, so after a few comments, we went about our own affairs—she to her kitchen to prepare breakfast for Jim and Father, and I to my computer. Each of us had a feeling of dread, because we knew that we would be facing the vampire's protégé for lunch.

Mother and I were seated in the sunroom patio when John drove up. A feeling of tenseness came over me as we waited for him. When he entered the glass door, he exclaimed in a rather loud voice, "I have great news, Mother. Rosemary has assigned me an angel."

I laughed, "An angel?"

Immediately John's face showed his disgust. "I wouldn't expect you to understand. The fallen never do!"

"Oh, my God," I moaned and looked out the window at the garden.

Mother, trying to be calm, said, "John, really now, you know we don't believe in a concept of angels on earth." When she noticed how her son squirmed, she added, "You know what I mean. Here on earth! We don't think that they are among us, do we?"

I interjected, "Mother's trying to say that we don't give angels a literal interpretation. They might be in heaven, but hardly here on earth."

"That's where you're both wrong. They are among us. Rosemary has assigned me my own personal angel."

"Is it here in the room with you?" I asked, dismayed.

"Certainly!" he asserted. "She is always with me, guiding me, helping me."

Mother and I looked at each other for a second. We were both astounded and did not know how to respond.

At last I asked, "Is that part of the Jesus Plan?"

"It sure is. When you are on the path set out for you, an angel is assigned for your protection and help."

"How does Rosemary assign them?" Mother asked.

"Oh, Mother, her Reverend-father has anointed her with the blessed duty of assigning angels. Rosemary is practically a saint. She has gone further than I can ever expect to go. Thank God we've come together."

"Does your angel have a name?" I asked.

"Certainly, but it will be revealed to me later."

"Why later?" Mother asked.

"I have to become worthy of her."

"When will you know that you are?" I asked.

"After I have proven myself to her, I'll be worthy."

"How do you do that?" Mother inquired.

"When I have sufficiently done what my angel has directed."

I interjected, "Don't you mean 'what Rosemary has directed'?"

John stiffened. "Don't you try to demean her. She has wisdom you'll never achieve."

Enough was enough! I stood up and stated, "John, you were never a good student. It was your ability in sports that always carried you through school. Now I see why you didn't make it in academic studies. You are so gullible, you'd believe anything."

Mother did not want an argument and took John by the arm. She said, "Dear son, let's you and I go into the family room and talk about it. You know our doubting Thomas is not going to agree with you." She winked at me and started leading John away.

"That's evident! He *is* a doubting Thomas. You sure gave him the right name," he exclaimed as he went with her.

I began eating my sandwich and gazed at the garden. Suddenly I started laughing—but not loudly. I found myself searching for an angel among the trees and flowers. When Mother and John returned, I was finishing my sandwich. They were talking about Rosemary, and Mother revealed that John's fiancée would join us for dinner that evening. That too struck me as funny. I don't know why, but I quickly stood up and ran into the house. I didn't want to further antagonize my brother.

After John departed, Mother asked me why I had laughed. I confessed that I had found the whole situation too preposterous for words. My only recourse in trying to understand the family's predicament was to laugh at it. John, in my opinion, had been brainwashed, and I feared that there was nothing we could do about it. Rosemary had so subjugated him that any reasoning or arguments we might put forward would be pointless. My comments upset Mother, and she ended our conversation by saying, "I'll talk with your father about it."

My impulse to laugh returned. My father was the last person on earth who could have challenged my brother's mind-set. Father was an artist of an earlier school. His artistic style was considered old-fashioned by critics. Yet his work sold because his paintings portrayed realistic scenes of Americana similar to Norman Rockwell's. He knew that he would never be a great artist and did not care. He could not go along with modern art trends. He did not have the force of character needed by the artist who envisions new directions. So, how could such a gentle, fine man combat a force as threatening as Rosemary? I was sure he could not. That meant that the burden was definitely falling on me—and I didn't have an angel!

As the evening approached, the Whitney family once again became tense. We did not discuss our problem, but each of us acted outside our usual behavior. Father mentioned that for some reason he had not been able to paint that day. He just had no inspiration. Mother was bothered by the fact that she had not buttered the glass pie plate that she had used for the evening dessert. Twice she said, "I fear the pie won't come out in very attractive pieces." Jim managed to be invited to a close friend's house for the evening. I became anxious. Facing the vampire was a fearful thought. It would be our second confrontation, and she had proved that nothing fights back like ignorance. No matter what I would say, she would hide behind the Holy Bible. Her quotations from the holy book rarely answered my questions, but she always seemed in control by spouting out some high-sounding phrase. The prospects for the evening were not pleasant.

When the engaged couple entered our home at six o'clock that evening, it was obvious that Rosemary was ready for contention. We were not greeted with her usual sickly-sweet smile. Instead we were accosted by her Evil Eye, which glistened pointedly and menacingly. I had an urge to step backward to avoid her gaze. She was prepared. Even before we were all seated in the family room, she started her campaign. It was like having a fifth horse in the biblical Apocalypse.

As Rosemary walked toward the fireplace, she asked in a rather unnatural voice, "Where do you want the accused to sit?"

We were all taken aback. When she stopped and looked at us for direction, her demeanor was savage. No guest had ever entered the Whitney home in such a manner. Mother pointed to her own chair by the fireplace and softly answered, "See if you're comfortable in this one."

Without replying, Rosemary marched, head high, over to the chair and sat down. John joined her in a nearby chair. The rest of the family fell into the seats closest to where they were standing. Later, I realized what a brilliant tactic the vampire had used. We were all taken off guard by her clever disconsolation. Directing her Evil Eye at me, Rosemary said, "I suppose you are the one who has upset my dearest John, your brother."

I decided to be flippant. "Oh, is he upset?"

She gasped like a dragon preparing to exhale flame, "Such nerve!" Her eyes burned into me.

John interjected, "Tom, be respectful!"

Father, who had been quietly listening, suddenly said, "Now let's all calm down."

I could not be calm. "Is she being respectful?" I quickly asked.

John could not answer, but Rosemary could. "Listen, young man, you are in danger of hellfire!"

"Oh?" I questioned, sitting up as if I were surprised. "I don't feel the least bit warm."

Rosemary looked at John as if he should do something about the way I was responding. It was as if she wanted an argument and I was not being cooperative.

John raised his voice. "Tom, we did not come here for your rude behavior. You have brought doubt into our family's heart, and Rosemary and I mean to clear it up."

Mother interceded. "Perhaps we should have dinner now and then continue our discussion?"

"No, not now!" John replied. "I want Tom to behave. He's not going to criticize my future wife without apologizing."

Again I sat up. My face must have shown my puzzlement. "When did I criticize your fiancée?" I turned toward Rosemary and asked, "Do you feel that I owe you an apology?"

She was not expecting my question and again looked at John.

"Yes, she does, and if you'll do it, we'll have dinner."

I shrugged my shoulders. If a few words would clear up the stalemate, I did not care one way or the other; so I said, "If I've offended you in any way, I do apologize."

Rosemary raised her head to show her condescension, then turned to Mother and said in a tone of false kindness, "I think dinner would be a fine idea."

We adjourned to the dining room. Once seated, Rosemary turned toward the head of the table and asked, "Were you told about Tom's attitude in regards to John's marrying me?"

Father looked at the fork he had picked up, studied it a moment, and then answered, "Yes, I was told."

"Then before we offer prayer for our dinner, I think we should briefly discuss the problem that Tom seems to perceive."

Everyone was quiet, so I broke the silence by saying, "Rosemary, my parents have invited us to the table for dinner. Let's have the discussion afterward, please."

The Evil Eye was directed toward my father, but he remained reticent.

I continued. Looking at Rosemary, I said, "May I ask you to deliver our evening prayer?"

It was a clever move on my part, even though I had not planned it. She could not pass up an invocation to prayer, so she nodded.

"Lord Jesus, forgive the unkindness that dwells in the heart of one of your disciples. Let him understand his perilous stance and no more doubt your word. May peace return to this wonderful family!"

It really was more than I could endure. She was the cause of the discord in our family, and she was blaming me. Such nerve! How I found the resolve to do it, I don't know, but I immediately said quite loudly, "And Lord Jesus, help us to stamp out the evil that has come into our family."

John, under the influence of the Evil Eye that quickly turned on him, let slip from his mouth, "Damn you!"

Mother and Father both exclaimed in piteous tones, "John!"

Rosemary started to stand up but stopped when Mother said, "My dear, please stay. We must discuss this matter rationally. We simply have to!"

Clearly against her wishes, she hesitated, but she sat when John took her arm and guided her back into her chair. He said, "My darling, we must let them understand our happiness in the Lord. What you have done for me is so different from what we are used to. Please help me to explain our covenant as you have revealed it to me."

Rosemary nodded but did not look at me.

Mother said, "Thank you for your prayer, Rosemary. Now let me pass the roast beef. I'm sure you've noticed, Rosemary, that in this household we mainly eat beef, because Father doesn't care for chicken or pork."

Trying to ease the tenseness of the situation, Father commented, "Yes, I've never liked chicken or pork, because those animals eat everything they come upon."

Rosemary actually gave Father a short, kind smile.

Mother continued passing dishes to the right around the table, and the family began eating quietly. The silence did not remain for long.

For reasons I cannot explain, I simply had to continue upsetting Rosemary. I think it was because I felt that I had her on the run. She was greatly distressed, in my opinion, that she had not been able to vanquish the entire family with her planned entrance performance. I had interrupted it, which meant that things hadn't gone the way she wanted. At the table, her effort to attack me in her prayer had only brought on a rebuttal that incensed her. So, I increased her hatred one hundred percent by asking, "John, is your angel with you today?"

No one spoke. John and his fiancée could only stare at each other. Suddenly, Rosemary looked skyward and opened the oracle: "Lord Jesus, save this sinner from the evil that dwells among us."

"A capital idea, "I interjected.

At that, John started to stand, but this time Rosemary pulled him back down. Turning toward me with blazing eyes, she stammered out, "Yes, his angel is with him, and pray God she will always be with him."

Mother tried passing a dish of potatoes, but no one paid any attention.

Trying to be facetious, I said, "I like the concept of a guiding angel. I have great admiration for cupids. What wonderful creatures they would be to have around. Just think: You could say to the little fellow, 'Fly off and bring me a glass of water.' And the little bugger would do it. Wouldn't that be great?"

Rosemary was ready for argument. "How do you dare compare something like that with an angel?"

"Well, they're both good ideas but, of course, impractical. You'd have to pay the cupid's health insurance and his social security. It's just not practical today. Does one have to do that for an angel?"

"Oh, Lord Jesus, help this poor sinner."

John added, "Tom, you've lost your soul."

"I hadn't noticed," I responded.

Rosemary and John looked at each other in desperation. It was as if they were asking each other whether they should leave or not.

"Oh, no!" Mother said, sensing their reaction. Tears began falling from her eyes, and she raised her hands to wipe them away. "

Father said in a tone I had never heard, "Tom, apologize!"

I did, immediately, and John and Rosemary relaxed and continued eating.

We ate in silence. When we finished, Mother collected our dishes and brought out her apple pie. It restarted the conversation. Everyone praised her dessert, after which we retired to the family room.

When Father began talking, it seemed as if he was seeking preeminence over the group, a trait not often shown in his character. Yet it was evident that he wanted to be assertive. He mentioned problems that can arise in a marriage if there are misunderstandings from the beginning. He felt that financial matters should be well-planned, that mutual interests should be obvious, and that the question of faith should be agreed upon. Mother tried speaking, but Father waved her down.

Turning to Rosemary and John, who were seated on the couch before him, he said, "You've known each other a very short time. You seem to have mutual interests, and perhaps you've discussed your finances, but the latter problem of faith has not, in my opinion, been solved. John, you were reared in the Presbyterian Church, which does not accept a literal interpretation of the Bible. Rosemary, you are a member of a church that does. This is just one aspect of the overall dilemma. You, John, seem to have accepted Rosemary's church wholeheartedly." John nodded. "And you, Rosemary, seem to have dominated his thinking in this regard." She started to talk, but Father waved her down too. "The major question now is whether John will be content in changing his faith to such an extent."

When Father finished, I was amazed that he had been so forthright and had presented the problem so well.

Rosemary spoke out first. "Father Whitney, you are correct. John has fully accepted my father's church, and I think he's found great contentment in doing so."

Mother added, "He seems very sincere and pleased."

Father said, "Yes, he does, and I ask only one thing. John, will you speak with our minister about your newfound religion? Surely that would not be asking too much?"

In a tone that showed her disapproval, Rosemary said, "Oh, I don't think he needs or wants such a confrontation. Do you, John?"

My brother hesitated and then said, "No. I don't see the need."

To my great surprise, Father did not back down. He asked, "But if I ask you to do it for me?"

Rosemary looked at John and slightly shook her head, showing her disapproval.

Before John could answer, Mother kindly begged, "Oh, do that for your father, John."

My brother looked at his fiancée and whispered quite audibly, "I must do it." Then he turned to Father and agreed.

Rosemary was not pleased and sat back in a huff.

Everyone noticed her behavior but pretended not to. I knew it was an example of what John would have to live with for the rest of his life, and I felt an urgency to halt the marriage. I said, "Be sure and tell Reverend Miller about your angel."

Rosemary sat back up and said, "John, I think we'd better go. I don't care for your brother's disparaging remarks about your newfound faith."

Bravely, I continued. "Rosemary, how do you have the power to assign an angel to someone?"

She stood up, looked at me venomously, and said, "I didn't come here to be insulted."

Mother spoke up. "Tom is only teasing, Rosemary. You'll get used to him, I'm sure."

John shook his fist at me and said, "He's not teasing. He's being sarcastic." He paused and added, "You'd better watch yourself, brother. I won't let you upset her again."

There was no way of saving the evening. The engaged couple quickly departed, even though Mother and Father both asked them to stay. I'll never forget the look that Rosemary gave me when she left the room. Her eyes were those of a demon. How Hollywood could have used them!

Mother and Father both reproached me for my conduct during the evening, but I defended myself. "I was merely trying to make John wake up!"

"It's too late for that," Mother said.

"I'm not sure," Father stated. "He did promise to talk with Reverend Miller, and I believe that's what he needs. We can hope that our minister can make John see that the literal interpretation of the Bible in the Jesus Plan is not acceptable in our church. The Bible was made by human beings and is therefore capable of error. Our church recognizes that historical fact; the Jesus Plan doesn't. Let's hope Mr. Miller can make John understand the difference between the church he was reared in and the one he is entering."

Our family settled down for a quiet evening. No one wanted further discussion. Father worked on rearranging a shelf of art books, Mother sat in her chair by the fireplace mantel and read a magazine, and I started up my computer in the technical corner of the family room to watch the international news. When Jim returned from his friend's home, he asked what had transpired during Rosemary's visit. No one felt like reviewing the arguments that had occurred, but Father did say that John had agreed to talk with the family minister, Mr. Miller.

"He might as well talk to a stump," Jim said and laughed.

Mother put down her reading and said, "Jim, how disrespectful."

"Well, it's true. All of us in my Sunday school class make fun of him. He's just not cool."

"What do you mean," Mother asked.

Jim sat down on the couch before her. "He's always giving some historical point of view about Christ, and it sometimes contradicts what he's been preaching. When we question him, he gets befuddled, and we never really find out what he's been trying to say. Like the time he said that St. Paul was at the last supper. Historically, he couldn't have been, and my friend Henry called him on it. Mr. Miller avoided the proof."

"We can all get things mixed up," Mother said.

Father interrupted. "He means that our church does not give a literal interpretation of the Bible. We try to put things into a historical perspective. It's a much more reasonable approach in these modern times than interpreting the Lord Jesus as the man next door who can answer questions for you."

"Yeah," Jim agreed. "He'll only confuse John even more."

"Oh, mercy!" Mother exclaimed. "What are we to do if our own minister can't help us?"

"Well, I'm going to bed and watch TV," Jim said as he rose and left the room.

The rest of the family resumed their previous activity. To our surprise, John soon drove up the driveway. "He's home early," Mother commented, and we all turned and looked out the window facing the garage. When John entered, everyone stopped what they were doing and waited for an explanation of his early arrival.

"Good evening, everybody!" John greeted us. "I know you're surprised that I'm home so early, but there's nothing serious about it. Rosemary had a headache, so we called it a night."

"We're so glad to have you with us, dear boy," Mother said as John leaned over and kissed her forehead.

"Well, we thought it would also give me a chance to talk with you." He sat down on the couch across from Mother. Father joined them in his easy chair nearby. "You see," John continued, "I understand why you are upset with me, but I don't think you quite realize what Rosemary is doing for me."

"I think we do," I sarcastically blurted out, leaving my computer and joining them near the fireplace.

"No, you don't," John said in a kind rebuttal. "You see, I have not told you much about my experiences in Iraq when I was in the army."

"No, you haven't, and that has worried us," Mother confessed.

"Well, I've decided that I must tell you some things that happened to me in order to make you understand why I am now so content with Rosemary."

"This should be good," I said, teasing.

"Even you, Tom, might understand a bit, and you won't want to tease me like you've been doing."

I saluted him without comment.

"When I first got to Iraq, I went to Sunday services in the camp church. I tried to keep my faith in Christ, but events kept making me doubt my faith. In my third week there, I was sent out on patrol. I was with three buddies from my tent, and we were walking through a dirty, clay-walled village. Suddenly there was a terrific blast, a noise from hell, and a blinding light. The concussion threw me against a wall. I slid down on the ground and was unconscious for a few minutes. As I came to, I found that my hands had something mushy on them." John stopped and held back some tears. I felt terrible for having teased him. After he took out his handkerchief and wiped his eyes, he continued. "It was my buddy's brains."

We were all silent. What could one say?

John again gained control of himself and said, "He was lying over my legs and his head was burst open over me." Again he became tearful as he shook his head and looked at the floor.

Mother stood, walked to her son, and enclosed his head in her apron. He cried. Patting his head, she said, "John, that's enough. We simply did not know what you endured."

"Yes, son," Father said. "Only I wish you had told us earlier."

I added, "Me too, John,"

He sat back on the couch before starting again. "No, there was another incident that I want you to know about."

"We could wait, John," I suggested.

"No, it was the major reason for my being so confused when I returned. You can't imagine what life is like over there. It's another world, and I wasn't ready for it. I tried to hold onto my faith, but Christ did not mean much to me after what I saw. The kind beatitudes he preached had little meaning in a world of filth, hunger, and blood. How could God allow such suffering? What did Christ's message of love have to do with a battlefield? I was practically out of my mind. Surely you noticed how upset I was when I came home."

"Yes, we did," Mother said, "but we felt you had to accustom yourself to your old life and . . ."

When she hesitated, I said, "We thought you'd tell us in time what was bothering you. You were just so quiet."

He nodded. "Yes, I couldn't let it out. Somehow I wanted to protect you from the horrors I saw, but they had caused me to stop living. I could not find myself. Nothing seemed to matter. Surely you noticed?"

"Of course, we did," Father said, "but as your Mother said, we felt you should adjust yourself to your old life again. We didn't want to pry."

"I was thankful that you didn't. I couldn't have talked about anything at first. Everything here was so alien. I sort of had to start all over in learning how to live, and I was having a very difficult time of it. Then Rosemary came into my life. I swear I would have perished if she had not saved me."

We were all quiet. It was as if understanding of John's predicament had suddenly come to us. He had been miserable and was easy prey for a dominating force like Rosemary. At that moment, I believe we realized that we could not change his mind. Whatever was to come, John was lost to us forever.

Composed, John related another incident. He was on another patrol in the same village. "We heard planes zooming in on us. There were occasional mistakes. Improper wiring or timing sometimes led to disaster. We could hear bombs dropping. One exploded on a house just up from us. We were almost blinded by the flash but remained standing.

When the smoke cleared, we ran ahead, only to be met by a mother carrying a bloodied, wounded child out of the wreckage. She was hysterical. It was so pathetic, I had to turn away to hide my tears. We could not understand what she was saying, but it seemed like she was blaming us, screaming at us as if we'd done it. She too was bleeding, and we radioed for emergency aid. It quickly came, but it was too late for the child. The mother would not let go of her dead daughter and continued screaming." John stopped and wiped his tears. "I still hear her. I'll never forget it."

Never had our family felt so close. I was ashamed of my conduct in trying to awaken John to the power that was dominating him. He was inviting domination. He wanted the security of something to believe in. Circumstances were all on the side of the vampire, and we had lost him to her.

Mother comforted her son for a while and then said, "John, let's all go to the farm this coming weekend. Do you think Rosemary would go?"

He was silent for a while, then answered, "She might. I've not told her much about the farm. Perhaps she'd like to see it."

"Wonderful," Mother exclaimed. "Now, let's all go to bed. Tomorrow we'll discuss the weekend."

Everyone agreed, and the family retired. Mother had eased the situation by her idea of a weekend sojourn. She had inherited the farm, and we often went there in the summer. We had a cabin on the Sangamon River, and there was a pond for swimming and fishing on the farm. It seemed like the very thing we needed.

"No more this evening," Father said and started out of the room. The rest of us followed. At the staircase Mother kissed John and hugged him tightly. "Forgive us, my boy. We just did not know."

"Please, Mother, don't think about it. I would not want you to ever see the horror and cruelty that I witnessed. I am just glad that you now comprehend why I am content and why I am marrying Rosemary."

"Of course, my darling," she whispered. "Goodnight!"

John and I went up to our bedrooms. When we passed Jim's door, he called out, "Goodnight!"

I yelled back to him, "Don't kid me. I know you're going to stay up and watch some technical thriller."

"Thanks for the idea!" he answered.

At John's door I apologized for my past behavior, and he waved his hand as if it was forgotten. I said, "Thanks, John. And when we get to the farm, I'll show Rosemary where you shot your first rabbit."

He smiled and said, "I just hope she'll go with us. I'd like for her to see it. We've had a lot of fun there."

We parted. The next day when John came back from the Jesus Plan Church, he informed us that Rosemary had agreed on a weekend at the farm. We were all greatly pleased. Since the weekend was two days away, John had a chance to carry out his Father's wish and visit with Reverend Miller, the minister of the church we had attended all our lives. He was a short little man and overweight. He had a pleasant personality and saw everything through rose-colored glasses. Consequently, he was usually quite jovial and eager to please. Our family was surprised when he appeared at our door on the morning we were to leave for the farm. He had visited with John and wanted to talk with us.

In the family room where we gathered, Mr. Miller did not seem himself. He was not smiling, nor did he tell some amusing gossip about one of the church members. He first asked if he could speak frankly about John, because he was worried about him. He explained that after his visit with our ex-soldier, he had concluded that John was trying to escape from reality. "But you see," Miller implored, "it is not a healthy escape. One can be imaginative or industriously interested in a project to avoid the world, but when one loses all sense of proportion by losing oneself in an exaggeration of the most basic tenets of a religion, it is a psychological problem. John is doing just that. He has been led down a narrow path so unrealistic that he cannot possibly discern reality from fantasy. An example would be his preposterous belief that his fiancée has appointed an angel for his guidance." Mr. Miller chuckled suddenly and added, "Wouldn't we all want such divine help?"

Father spoke up. "You have pointed out the very thing I wanted to confirm. Now that I find that you agree with our estimation of the problem, I ask you: What can be done about it?"

Mr. Miller looked at the ceiling and then the floor. "I wish I knew. I would say, though, that I think you must tread very lightly."

"I'm afraid it's too late," Mother said, repeating the conclusion she had already reached several times.

"Perhaps," Mr. Miller agreed, "but maybe there is something that is causing him to seek escape."

At that point, I entered into the conversation. I explained to Mr. Miller about John's horrific experiences in the Iraq war. The soulful little minister soon had tears in his eyes. Nodding, he said, "I feared it was something horrible. I think I'd recommend a psychiatrist."

"Rosemary would never let him go to one," Mother said, "and I don't know how we could convince him that he should."

"No," Father added. "He would not believe us, and he's working in that Jesus Plan Church, so he's becoming independent. How could we persuade him that he needs psychiatric help? His fiancée would block any such endeavor."

"We don't want to alienate him," Mother said.

Mr. Miller nodded his agreement. Then he said, "I fear that I cannot help you further. Please let me have some time to think about an approach to the situation. It will be very difficult. You know that the churches involved are not alike—quite distant as a matter of fact—so I fear that my hands are tied. I could go to Reverend Shane if you wished, but it would be a waste of time. Anything I would say to him would be misinterpreted as a criticism. Being wrong is something the ignorant can never accept. You see, I'm calling them ignorant. Heaven knows what they would call me!" Mr. Miller chuckled again.

Father thanked the minister for coming, and Mr. Miller left after offering to be available to us anytime we felt we needed him.

"That was pointless," Mother said as we watched him walk down the driveway. "We already knew that we had lost our son. We must now make the best of it."

Chapter 3

The Outing

For the first time that lovely spring, we went to our farm, Mother's heritage. It had always been a place of refuge for us in the summertime. There we did so many of the things young boys like to do. We played in the hayloft of the old barn; we swam in the pond and disturbed Father's fishing efforts; we climbed through the vales and dales of nearby Allerton State Park; and best of all, Mother's sister Aunt Lucy lived there. We loved her homemade bread and dark-brown applesauce. The place held many memories, and I was glad for a warm spring weekend in the country.

Mother, Father, Jim, and I left after Reverend Miller departed. We were eager to freshen up our cabin on the Sangamon River and have lunch with our widowed Aunt Lucy, who was expecting us. Rosemary and John would join us later that evening. The three-hour trip went quickly, and we arrived at the old farmhouse just as our dear grey-haired Aunt Lucy was setting a table for our lunch.

Tall, handsome cousin Charles, whom we had not seen for some time, was visiting, so there were many hugs, slaps on the back, and kisses before settling down for some nourishment. Charles had wavy black hair and was five years older than my brother John. They had been very close friends all of their lives.

Aunt Lucy's homemade bread was in abundance, as were the *ohs* and *ahs* when she served it. It seemed like old times, and I think our family especially enjoyed it because we were so relaxed. There was none of the tension we had been experiencing the last few days at home—at lease not yet.

Cousin Charles was Aunt Lucy's oldest son and her greatest worry. He was a ladies' man and had an uncontrollable appetite for sexy women, blonde or brunette. He had been married three times, and the second marriage had graced the world with two children, the darlings of Aunt Lucy's life. However, Aunt Lucy did not approve of divorce and agreed that her second daughter-in-law should raise the children.

This left Charles, a successful businessman, time for the chase. Women could not resist him, and he knew it. I was surprised that he did not have a prospective wife with him for our visit. His game of conquest usually employed the hint of a possible marriage. I had always enjoyed his company because of the sexual exploits and humorous incidents he would reveal when we were alone. I liked his *bon vivant* personality. Of all the times for my venal cousin to be visiting, it would be the day that Rosemary, the staunch virgin vampire, was coming with my brother.

After lunch we drove over to our cabin on the Sangamon River. Cousin Charles went with us and entertained us with memories from our past years at the farm—as well as some of his latest exploits with women. Mother twice had to mention that some things are best kept to oneself, and Charles always apologized for telling a rather raunchy tale.

We dusted the cabin, cleaned out any spider webs, and made the beds in the three loft bedrooms. I checked to make sure our rowboat had survived the winter and that our swing attached to a large oak limb still swung out over the water. Everything seemed in order. It was decided that Charles would stay with us in the cabin and sleep with Jim so that Rosemary and John could have the upstairs bedrooms in the old farmhouse with Aunt

Lucy. The cabin soon felt alive again after our cleanup efforts, and we returned to the farmhouse and Aunt Lucy.

The evening began with a bad start. When Rosemary arrived on the front porch, Aunt Lucy went out to meet her. The wrinkled little farm woman suddenly stopped in her tracks to see a beautiful lady fall to her knees, fold her hands in prayer, and seemingly give a blessing. Puzzled, Aunt Lucy looked at John who was standing behind his fiancée. "She's blessing your house," he told her. That only added to the little woman's confusion.

"Why?" Aunt Lucy asked.

"Just a minute," John whispered into the air.

As the rest of the family emerged from the house, they also noticed something peculiar and stood silent. Charles, however, came out, looked at Rosemary, and said, "Did you fall, honey?" He then walked over to her and raised her up on her feet.

"*Really*, sir!" Rosemary snapped, her Evil Eye penetrating into Charles face.

Taken aback, Charles apologized and said, "I just thought you needed help, Lassie."

Rosemary straightened her skirt and said, "I am not a Lassie!"

"Well, whatever you are, you sure are pretty," Charles said kindly and winked at her.

John stepped into the scene. "Charles, I want you to meet my fiancée, Rosemary."

"Well, I'll be damned. You sure picked a pretty one."

Rosemary's face showed her distress, and she addressed Charles coolly. "You need not try flattery with me. I know your wastrel type."

Charles laughed. 'Oh, you're too good to be true." Turning to John, he added, "Cousin, where did you find her?"

Rosemary walked by Charles without looking at him. She drew alongside Aunt Lucy, and the two entered the house. John quickly followed. When the new arrivals were inside, Charles asked me, "What's with her? A cob up the ass?"

I could not help but laugh and put my arm around my cousin. "Charles, you simply cannot believe just what kind of woman that is. She's a Jesus freak!" I laughed again and went into detail about my future sister-in-law. The more I revealed, the louder Charles shouted *no* in disbelief. He could hardly believe his ears. I swore that everything I was telling him was true and that our family had finally ceased our efforts to intercede.

"Well, let me at that sacred pussy!" Charles declared, and he went into the house.

I followed him, thinking, *Charles, you don't know what you're up against!* I laughed to myself. This was going to be good.

John had immediately led Rosemary into a front living room where they could be alone for a few minutes. I was sure he knew that his fiancée was terribly upset, and the entire visit could be ruined by Charles's teasing. I would have loved to have heard the conversation between them. They stayed away from the family for at least two hours—until it was time for dinner. Aunt Lucy knocked on the parlor door and invited them to the table in the dining room. They were seated together on a bench at one end.

Aunt Lucy folded her hands and said a short prayer. It was not enough, of course; so Rosemary apparently called on the Lord Jesus in silence, even after the hostess said, "Amen." Without a word to anyone, the vampire raised her face toward the ceiling for her own devotions. Paying no attention to her, Charles said, "Mother, it's just great to hear your sweet little prayers."

Aunt Lucy looked at her son and pointed a finger at Rosemary. Charles looked and shrugged his shoulders with a puzzled look. Everyone else was sort of frozen, afraid of offending the vampire; but when she finished, she sweetly said to the hostess, "I merely wanted to add a blessing for this wonderful family."

Charles coughed, but Aunt Lucy thanked Rosemary. "That was sweet of you, dear."

"Yes, one can never have enough prayer," Charles commented, but his laugh afterward showed his sarcasm.

Rosemary gave him a look that would have killed a tarantula, but it did not faze Charles, who added, "Clara, my second wife, could sure give a sincere prayer. Even our minister bowed to her prowess."

Mother asked Charles about his children, and he replied, "Oh, they're fine. You've never seen two prettier girls. Only problem is, that mother of theirs is making Jesus Freaks out of them."

Aunt Lucy reprimanded her son instantly by the tone of her voice: "Charles!"

"I think I have a headache," Rosemary said to John. "May I be excused?"

Aunt Lucy quickly pointed at her son and said, "My dear, don't pay any attention to him. He did not learn such bad manners here at home. Charles, please apologize to her."

"Sure!" Charles agreed. "And if it will cure that headache, I'll even write it down." When Rosemary closed her eyes as if she were displeased, Charles instantly realized he had gone too far. In a normal tone, he said, "I certainly did not mean to be disrespectful."

John patted his fiancée's hand, and she opened her eyes but did not look at Charles.

Father changed the subject. "I think I'll try fishing in the pond tomorrow."

"Joe's sons caught some beautiful bluegills yesterday," Aunt Lucy informed him.

A sort of smile formed on the vampire's face, and she said, "May he be blessed!"

Charles made a slight grunt, which caused his mother to look at him rather severely.

Again there was a hesitation in the conversation. Jim began it again. "Instead of fishing, let's go over to Allerton Park and have a run."

Charles and I agreed. Our family had a long association with the park where we had spent many hours of our childhood, running along the trails through the woods and dales. The park was famous in Central Illinois for the various activities that took place there, including running competitions and art exhibits.

"Be careful over there," said Aunt Lucy. "The Allerton Park Trail Run had a couple of accidents last fall during their trials. Those paths have roots and stones sticking out of them, and two people fell and seriously hurt themselves."

"We'll be careful," Jim said and laughed.

"Yes, you laugh," Aunt Lucy said with a grin, "but I'll laugh if you fall."

"I'll be very careful," he replied and winked at his auntie.

Rosemary turned to John and said, "I don't think I would like that, John. Do we have to go?"

Aunt Lucy spoke up. "Oh, there's plenty to do without taking a long walk. The gazebo there is now very popular for weddings. You would love it. It's so beautiful."

Rosemary smiled and said, "That might be pleasant."

"Fine," John quickly said. "We'll go there. I know you'll love it. It's really a very beautiful park."

It was settled. The young people would visit the park the next day.

Charles behaved himself for the rest of the meal, and the family—after many inquiries about certain relatives, who were described for Rosemary's benefit—went to the cabin. John and Rosemary stayed at Aunt Lucy's.

Driving over to the nearby cabin, Charles wanted more information about Rosemary. He could not believe that John, who had always been so athletic and fun to be with, could possibly be in love with that woman. "Gosh," Charles said. "No one could ever outrun John, and he could throw a football half a field. How can he love a woman who won't even go for a walk? Has she changed him that much?"

"I don't like her!" Jim blurted out.

I tried explaining our situation in regards to Rosemary, and Mother and Father added details.

"But what's that Jesus Plan?" Charles asked. "I get enough of Jesus when I visit my daughters. That ex-wife of mine has gone into one of those "saved-again" churches; they are so rank and ignorant, it's pathetic."

"Then you know what we're up against," I concluded.

"Yes, I do, and God help you!"

"We'll *need* His help," Jim said.

At the cabin, Charles and I had a beer and talked almost till midnight about our future sister-in-law. Charles was adamant that the wedding should be cancelled, but he had no workable suggestions on how that could be accomplished.

The next morning after breakfast, John and Rosemary drove over, and Charles, Jim, and I climbed into the backseat of their car. We departed for the family outing in the park. Mother and

Father stayed at the cabin so that Father could paint and Mother could do some cleaning. It was a beautiful spring day. Leaves were forming, which gave the woods a light-green brilliance in the sunlight. It was a perfect day for a companionable occasion.

On the way to the park, John suggested that we drive by the *Sun Singer*, a famous statue. Everyone agreed, and John asked Rosemary to read aloud to us from a brochure that Aunt Lucy had given him about the famous statue. "Yes, please do," I said, and Rosemary took the pamphlet and started reading.

"The *Sun Singer* is a seventy-five-year-old statue of the Greek god Apollo. It is fifteen feet tall and stands on a limestone pedestal. The statue was commissioned by Robert Allerton, then the owner of the estate with his life partner John Gregg."

Rosemary suddenly stopped reading and asked, "What does it mean by the phrase *life partner*?"

Charles, Jim, and I looked at each other. Charles started to laugh, but I put a finger to my lips.

Charles explained, "You know, when two men are in love."

Rosemary snarled and looked at John. "How could you want to show me a statue that belonged to two such men? Creatures like that are worse than vermin."

Charles made a face and bent over so he could laugh.

John, evidently without forethought, said, "Darling, in the Iraq war I saw a lot of men that had affairs with other men."

"What? Our soldiers did that sort of thing?"

"Well, no one thought anything about it. It was war, and everyone was tense and mixed up."

"I pray God that you didn't participate in that sort of sinful behavior."

Charles looked at Jim and me and acted as if he were crying. We were amused but kept silent.

"No, darling, I didn't." John continued, "But I had buddies who were very close companions. I'd say they were in love."

"Heavens! And you talked to them? You considered such vermin as buddies? How could you?"

Charles raised his middle finger and put it behind Rosemary's seat and mouthed the words, *Fuck you!*

John shook his head. "I guess you had to be there to understand. We were under terrible pressure. There wasn't such a thing as normality. Our world was turned upside down."

"What is there to understand? It must have been pretty obvious that they were breaking the laws of the Bible."

Charles pursed his lips and said silently, *Oh, no!* and made a face as if something disastrous had happened.

Impatient, John raised his voice and said, "The laws of the Bible are far from your mind when bombs are shattering the world around you."

The three of us in the back seat could hardly believe that John had dared speak up to her.

"Well, they shouldn't be," she said. "That's when you should be praying."

"We did pray—and most earnestly—but some found comfort in holding a buddy close." Tears came to John's eyes. "I had a buddy blown apart, and he fell on me. If he had lived, I would have hugged him very close."

The three of us in the back seat could hardly control ourselves from laughing, but we remained quiet. John was finally talking back to her, and we wanted to hear every word.

"What are you trying to tell me?" Rosemary demanded.

"Oh, for gosh sakes," John said. "There was nothing sinful in the closeness I felt for him. His brains were all over me. How would you feel?"

Rosemary was silent. They drove quietly for a while; then she continued reading.

"The statue was recently restored by Sculpture Sources of Chicago. They were able to sandblast the corrosion from the bronze of the figure and applied a blue-green patina, which was the original color of the statue. Robert Allerton had seen the work of the Swedish sculptor Carl Milles in Stockholm Harbor in 1929 and hired him as the creator of the *Sun Singer*."

John interrupted her reading. "Look. It's straight ahead. There's a drive around it, so we can see it from all angles." In a few moments, the car entered the circular drive, and John said, "Isn't that a remarkable thing? Imagine being able to sculpt something like that. My Father is a great admirer of it and has visited the gardens of Carl Milles in Stockholm."

Rosemary suddenly realized that nakedness was in full view and said, "What a blatant absence of morality."

Charles snickered, and I held Jim's mouth shut.

"But darling, it's a statue!" John said as if he could hardly believe what his fiancée had said.

Rosemary wanted to return to Aunt Lucy's, but John, in his usual submissive tone, pleaded with her to continue on. She agreed, but only if there were no more such revolting things in the park. Did she have some surprises ahead!

After parking, we discussed the various trails and decided to walk to the Mayan game arena. John assured Rosemary that it was not far, and the group set out. Charles, Jim, and I walked faster and were soon quite a distance from the happy couple. I was glad, because Charles started telling about his latest exploits and "conquests," as he called them, and some of the stories were very raunchy and naughty. Whether his tales were true or false didn't matter. He always entertained us, and we would have listened to anything.

As we approached the Mayan game arena, Charles asked, "Does Rosemary know that this estate once belong to two famous gay men who lived here all their lives?

"I doubt it," I answered.

"Wow, won't she have a fit when she finds out. What she needs is a good fuck."

Jim laughed, and I said, "Not too loud, Charles! They're not that far behind."

We walked up to the edge of the impressive sunken arena, noted for its accurate design of an ancient Mayan sports playground. The stone walls had bas-relief figures of naked men playing ball and running frantically in all directions. It was masterfully carved, and the canopy of oak limbs over the sides gave a finished touch to the scene.

Charles said, "Just imagine the host and his friend with their carload of Chicago faggots running around in the arena naked. I understand he sometimes transported pansies down for weekends. Course, the Mayans played the game very seriously. The losers were decapitated."

"Really?" Jim asked.

"Of course they gave each other blow jobs first." Charles laughed.

Again, I said, "Not so loud, Charles!"

John and Rosemary were with us in seconds. She asked, "Well, for goodness sake, what was that used for? It's almost as big as a football field."

"Well, a small one," John said and then explained. "They usually played a type of ball game in there, only they were very serious about it. The losers lost their lives."

"Oh, how horrible those heathens were!" she commented.

Charles disagreed. "Oh, I don't think so. They loved sports and put competitors to the highest test. Imagine how viciously you would fight if it meant your life?"

"Oh, such godlessness!" she exclaimed.

Charles wouldn't drop the subject. "Not really. They had a view of life different from ours. Besides, they probably enjoyed running around naked in this lovely oblong bowl. I wouldn't mind doing it myself. Let's all undress and play tag." He laughed.

Rosemary pulled John aside and whispered something to him. The couple turned away.

"Where are you going?" I asked.

"We'll meet you at the gazebo for lunch," John replied. "Have a good walk." He then escorted his fiancée back toward the path.

The rest of us decided that we'd run around in the arena a little and then go on down the path for a while. It really was fun to run and throw rocks in the air and catch them. Soon we were walking farther along the path, which followed along the side of a winding stream that buffeted interesting rock formations. It was quite beautiful with the water flowing so fast from the spring rains. About a half hour into the hike, we started our return. When we passed the Mayan arena again, Charles suggested that we return after lunch and have some kind of game. I liked the idea, but we were not much farther along when we saw John standing beside Rosemary, who was lying on her back on a broad rock formation. When he saw us, he called, "Help!"

We ran to them and found out the ghastly news. Rosemary had slipped on a rock and had twisted her ankle. She could not walk. Everyone expressed their sympathy, but Charles had a bad time of stifling a laugh. We decided that John and I would support the victim on either side and carry her to the gazebo. Charles and Jim walked on, while we slowly made our way along the path.

At the gazebo, our problems were even more complex. The building was set high up, with a winding staircase up to the floor. Inside were benches and fine views of the woods. I could also see very large stone Foo dogs, which, according to Chinese legends, were placed before important structures as guards. They were said to undergo a metamorphosis at night and become alive so they could watch over the estate. When Rosemary saw the staircase, she exclaimed, "Oh, no! I can't go up that!"

"We'll carry you just like we've been doing," John said. "After all, you've made it easily all the way up the path."

"No, I am not being carried up those stairs. We're going back to Aunt Lucy's now. Please!" It was final. John and I helped her to their car, and I told John that I would call our father on my cell phone to come for us. John nodded, and they quickly drove away, but not in the direction of the *Sun Singer*!

"She must have tripped over her angel," Charles said as they left, and laughed heartily.

I couldn't help but smile.

"Too bad she didn't break her neck," Jim said.

"Don't be so severe," Charles teased. "You might end up liking her."

"Never!" Jim assured us.

"Well, just wait till she puts her Evil Eye on you. You'll change your mind."

I interrupted their banter. "Will you two stop! Let's have lunch!"

We took the food Aunt Lucy had prepared for us up on the gazebo and sat down at a table where the view was especially fine. One could see rows of blue hyacinths and groups of blooming daffodils among the bright-green foliage.

As we talked, Charles suddenly said, "It wasn't that bad a sprain. Bet that bitch makes John take her to a doctor.

"I doubt it," I replied.

"Bet she did! Any bets?"

"Oh, all right, I'll bet you," I said. "How much?

"First night with your first wife!"

"You bastard!" I joked. "Only you would think that up!"

That afternoon we returned to the Mayan arena and raced each other for a short period. Somehow the festive nature of our outing had been destroyed by the vampire's fall, so when Father came for us, we decided that we'd return to Aunt Lucy's and find out if John needed us for anything. When we arrived, we found out that I had lost the bet. John had taken Rosemary to a doctor's office in the nearby town of Monticello.

It was early evening before John and the patient returned. Rosemary's foot was tightly bound in tape, and she walked from their car on one foot with John holding her up. She wanted an immediate departure for home, but John, with Mother's help, convinced her that it was too late for such a drive. "Do wait until morning," Mother earnestly pleaded.

Rosemary finally consented but gave John a look of great dissatisfaction. I couldn't help but think that she would make him miserable for not doing what she wanted. Yet I thought that if his refusal dissolved their engagement, so much the better. When it was time for dinner, Rosemary asked if she could have a plate in her bedroom. Aunt Lucy obliged. The rest of us gathered at the table, and to our surprise, John asked if he could give the blessing. Aunt Lucy nodded, and John looked skyward. The rest of us looked at each other. My mind drifted. *Oh, no! She's got him doing it their way. Ugh!* John started slowly. It was obvious that he was a novice, but he did utter some phrases that sounded like something his fiancée would have thought up. He concluded with "Amen."

"John, since when did you start saying prayers at the table?" Charles asked in a jovial voice, smiling.

"It is rather new for me," John admitted, "but you see, in the Jesus Plan, one has to be capable of prayer for many occasions."

With a smirk, Charles asked, "Does one have to be in the Jesus Plan—whatever it is?"

John replied resolutely. "For true meaning in life, it's the best thing I've found yet."

"But you were reared in a church. What's the difference?" Charles inquired, looking rather puzzled.

John hesitated. It seemed that he was having trouble differentiating between his family's religion and the Jesus Plan."

Mother helped him by kindly teasing, "Oh, Charles, that's an awfully serious question for someone during dinner. Why don't you discuss it afterward?"

Jim asked, "What are we doing this evening?"

"Let's play cards like we used to," I suggested.

"That's a plan!" Charles agreed. "What'll we play?"

"How about pinochle?" Father proposed.

John, suddenly downcast, said, "I don't think I'm allowed to play cards. It's just not accepted by the Jesus Plan, you know."

"Jesus!" Charles burst out. "I'm surprised they let you breathe!"

"Charles, be kind," Mother said.

"Well, I didn't want to play pinochle anyway," Charles admitted. "I haven't played that in ages. Let's play blackjack."

"No, let's play *Monopoly*," said Jim.

Charles laughed. "That's an old one. Mother, do we still have my old *Monopoly* set here?"

Aunt Lucy nodded. "It's upstairs in the hall closet."

All the men except Father were soon sitting around the dining room table engrossed in the game. John could not play cards, but evidently a game was allowed. When Charles's hat token landed on something harmful, he would shout an expletive; and Aunt Lucy, sitting with Mother and Father in the parlor, would call out, "Not so loud!"

After some time and many laughs and shouts, Rosemary called rather weakly from the top of the stairs, "John, may I see you a moment?" He immediately left the game and went to her bedroom. The men paused their play, thinking that he would return soon, but it was twenty minutes or so before he came down the steps.

Approaching the table, John said, "I shouldn't be playing that game. Gambling is not in the Jesus Plan."

Charles laughed. "Well, I'll never take you to Las Vegas!"

John smiled, but went back upstairs.

Charles shook his head and said in a low voice, "Can one take a dump in the Jesus Plan, or is that not allowed?"

"Now you really understand what we're up against, don't you?" I said.

"I sure do," he replied, "but I sure as hell don't know what you're going to do about it."

The interruption of the game spoiled the fun, and we quit playing. We returned to the cabin where Jim drank a Coke and Charles and I drank beer, which, of course, would certainly not be in the Jesus Plan.

The next morning after breakfast, Charles and I went over to Aunt Lucy's. He asked John if he would mind discussing his newfound religion with him. "I must admit," he said, "that I'm terribly curious about it. Let's go outside and sit down and talk." When John agreed, Charles and I accompanied him out on a screened-in porch. As we sat down on a sofa, Charles said, "John, you were always my favorite cousin. We were close in age, and we played together. But now you seem like a different person. We always had so much fun playing baseball or football when we were out here. Gosh, I swear that you knew every trail in the park. But now you don't seem allowed to do anything. What's happened to you?"

John looked downcast. Finally he answered. "Maybe I've grown up. I don't seem to need all that frivolous stuff anymore."

"There was nothing frivolous in our activities," Charles protested. "We had great times playing games in the park and swimming in the lake. What's wrong with all of that?"

"Oh, I'm not saying there's anything wrong with what we used to do," John replied. "I'm just . . . well, I'm just too busy these days for games."

"What are you doing?"

"I work in the Jesus Plan. I serve as an accountant, and I help with various programs in the church."

Charles leaned back and turned toward John, "But you don't want to be a minister?"

"I don't know. I'll be whatever the Plan leads me to."

Charles had heard enough. "John," he burst out, "you've got to think again about your fiancée. That woman is changing you, and I don't like what she's doing to you."

"Oh, she's wonderful," John refuted. "She's really helped me a lot."

"Well, what's this idiotic idea about you having an angel?"

"But I do!"

Charles laughed. "Oh, John, come to your senses. If I told you that I had an angel following me around, what would you say?"

"I'd be glad."

"No, you wouldn't. You'd say, 'What are you drinking these days?'"

John remained quiet.

I stayed out of the conversation; Charles was asking questions that our family had not dared to ask because we were afraid of offending John.

Charles continued. "Listen, John, I know women. That Rosemary is trying to dominate you, and you're falling for it. I swear it will get to the point where you won't be able to fart without her permission." John started to talk, but Charles wouldn't let him. "No, don't try to protect her. I've seen enough. Besides, she won't want to have a good fuck without a prayer beforehand."

John stood up. "Charles, that's none of your business."

Charles pulled his cousin back down on the sofa. "Listen, buddy, I know women. Rosemary will be so frigid, you'll never have a decent sex life."

John turned away, but Charles reached over and pulled him back. "Besides that, I think she's a class A hypochondriac. She'll have headaches and everything else all of your lives. She's the sort that thrives on doctor visits and taking medicine. You're heading for a hell on earth."

John quickly stood up and walked to the screen wall that surrounded the porch. He looked out at the forest. Then, looking back at Charles, he said, "You weren't in Iraq. You didn't see what

I saw. It was oblivion. I became worthless. I saw how cheap and meaningless life can be. I needed something to hang on to. You didn't see it, so you couldn't know. Rosemary is helping me. I'm beginning to think I have a purpose on this earth. I lost my desire for life in Iraq, but I'm finding it now. Please try to understand and don't goad me."

Charles stood and walked over to his cousin. "John, you know I care for you. Everything I said was for your benefit. Surely you can find yourself another way. Go to college! You've got the GI Bill."

"Aw, Charles, I know your intentions are good, but I think I'm on the right track. Let me find out, please."

Charles nodded and walked away. Then he suddenly turned and asked, "John, would you let me talk with Rosemary?"

"Of course, if she'll talk with you," John responded. "I'll ask her." He went into the house.

Charles turned to me and said, "What a bitch that poor guy's going to be stuck with!"

I nodded.

To my great surprise, Rosemary, holding onto John, came out on the porch and kindly said, "Charles, I understand you'd like to talk with me. We don't have much time, but I would be glad to discuss the Jesus Plan with you."

"Thank you, my dear. Let's sit down. I do want to talk with you, but I warn you, you won't like my questions."

A smirk appeared on her face as she selected a chair. "I'm not afraid of you. I've got God on my side."

Charles smiled. "Don't be too sure. You see, I've met your type before. My wife is so-called *born-again*. In order to vanquish my wife, I prepared quite thoroughly. I might be a lout and a drunk, but I've studied plenty."

Rosemary smiled quite confidently. "And so have I. You see, the devil is always lurking around, trying to—as you put it—*vanquish* the innocent. I too am prepared."

Charles bowed his head. "Now that we've both identified ourselves, let's start. My first question is, "Why did God wait so long before sending Jesus to our so-called *wicked* earth?"

"God sent his Son to redeem us from our sins."

"If God created us, why didn't he send Christ first so that all the humans in history would have his grace?"

"God saw his creation turn to sin and had to save us."

"If God is so all-powerful, why did He create a creature that can sin? Why didn't He make us perfect?"

"He did, and in His own likeness."

Charles smiled. "If he had made us perfect, Eve would not have offered the forbidden apple to Adam."

Rosemary snapped back, "God was testing us!"

"Why? Doesn't that show that he failed when he created us? His product wasn't perfect after all."

"Oh, that's just playing with words."

"And what about Jesus?"

"What do you mean?"

"Why didn't God send Jesus to India instead of the Middle East? There were a great many more sinners down on the Ganges than there were in the desert of Palestine."

Rosemary had no answer. She looked at John and said, "Ridiculous questions."

Charles responded, "Then answer this: Is God all-powerful and the personification of wisdom?"

"Tell him," John said to his fiancée.

"Of course, He is. That's a question for a child."

"Well, if God is so wise, why did he put the heads of three great religions in one place—I refer to Jerusalem—when he knew that they simply could not get along. He would have known that they all worshipped and interpreted him in different ways, and that such an arrangement could only lead to strife and bloodshed. He should have sent Jesus to India and Mohammed to China, and let the Jews have Jerusalem. Just think of what peace we'd have on earth!"

"Oh, you're just mixed up. The world was created by God, and its just the way it should be. The Bible tells us that."

"You're not answering my questions. Besides, the Bible is full of errors and contradictions; it's far from being a book of wisdom."

Rosemary sighed and, shaking her head, looked at John. "The Bible is perfect, and you are sacrilegious to think otherwise."

Charles shook his head. "Oh, dear, you've not studied the history of the Bible. Its creation was over a long period of time and conjured in a hocus-pocus manner."

Indignant, Rosemary's voice rose, "How dare you. That's blasphemy. The Bible is sacred and every word is true." She looked at John. Her eyes opened wide, and he nodded.

Charles smiled and shook his head. "Well, this is getting us nowhere. You don't answer my questions. You can't."

I expected that Rosemary would leave, but she did not. Instead she said, "If you didn't ask such childish things, I would answer." Then she straightened up and faced Charles as if she were a medieval knight before a dragon. "God is still on my side! Do you surrender?"

Charles laughed. "You're like my wife. Your ignorance is so great, there's no point in trying to discuss religion with you. And the worst part of it is, you don't see how ignorant you are."

A laugh came out of Rosemary's throat that reminded me of a dragon's tongue in religious pictures. Then she said, "Oh, a sinner always whines when cornered. You call me ignorant when I have the greatest power of all on my side." She laughed her fiendish laugh again.

"You have nothing but ignorance and supposition."

"And you have only incredulity. No faith at all!"

"That's the word I've been waiting for. The cornered always use faith as their defense. Merely by saying, you have to have faith, you would deny any proven fact if it contradicted something in the Bible. Well, you won't get off that easy with me."

Rosemary smiled sweetly. "It is a matter of faith. One's faith can see one through all the devil's efforts to deceive and mislead. Unfortunately for you, the devil has won."

Charles asked, "Are you saying that because I don't believe as you do, I'm a lost sinner?"

"Most assuredly!"

"Then you aren't a Christian. You are judging me. Isn't that against the rules?"

"You talk of rules. I am living Christ's commandments."

"No, you're not. I'm a much better Christian than you are."

A look of disbelief showed on Rosemary's face.

"Yes, I am," Charles continued. "You see, I know what Christ stands for."

"And what is that, in your view?"

"For the virtues that God gave his creatures! If we followed the principles of knighthood, we'd be Christlike."

"What are you talking about?"

"The seven virtues: faith, hope, charity, prudence, justice, fortitude, and temperance."

I admired Charles for spelling them out so easily and quickly. He told me later that he had used them with his wife repeatedly and could say them even when he was drunk.

Rosemary quickly responded. "See, you dare mention faith."

"Not in the way you use it as a cover for your ignorance. Your virtues are in the seven deadly sins."

Offended, Rosemary asked, "What do you mean by that?"

Charles answered quickly. "You show incredible pride in being superior to everyone because you're in the so-called Jesus Plan."

Rosemary raised her voice and in vociferous tones said, "Don't call the Jesus Plan *so-called*!"

"Well, you call it what you wish, but you have other sins acting as virtues. You just showed your wrath. Your ignorance keeps you from being an honest human being."

She blurted out, "You don't even know me!"

"Oh, yes I do! You demean Christ by the way you use him. You use him as a shield to hide your selfishness and your domination of others."

Rosemary turned to John. "I don't care for any more insults. Now he says I'm not honest."

"You're not," Charles pressed. "You judge, condemn, and hold yourself higher than others. You're a ghastly snob."

Rosemary faced John. "Are you going to let that lout say things like that to me? Where's your faith?"

John spoke up. "Charles, old buddy, you're being awfully rude. I think we'd better stop talking. We have to drive home, you know."

Charles looked at John and said, "Well, cousin, don't you see now what she's doing to you? Christ for her is just a means for domination. For your sake, I hope I've made an inroad into her distortion of Christ's message for mankind. I just pray you open your eyes and wake up."

Rosemary's head went up as she turned away, saying, "What nerve! As if God would listen to his prayers!" She turned to Charles and said, "Our conversation has shown that we have no common meeting ground. You do not have faith; I do. You misinterpret the Bible; I don't. There is no reason for any more discussion. I know that you wanted to show John the fallacy of the Jesus Plan, but God was triumphant. You have nothing to offer, where as I can lead him to eternal life." She haughtily raised her head and began limping away. John followed.

Aunt Lucy and Mother came out on the porch when it appeared that the young couple was leaving. "Anything happen?" Mother whispered to me.

I whispered back. "Yes! Plenty!"

The ladies and I walked out to John's car. Rosemary blessed us while thanking us for the care and comfort we had given her. John kissed both ladies, shook my hand, and joined the vampire. They drove away slowly. John waved, but Rosemary had her hands clasped in prayer and did not look out. As we walked back to the house, the ladies talked about the couple.

Aunt Lucy shook her head. "That dear boy. I am so afraid that he's in for trouble with her."

Mother said, "Oh, Lucy, I am just about worried to death. John is such a wonderful boy. Everyone has always liked him, and he always had so many friends. She just doesn't seem the type of wife he should have."

"She isn't!" Lucy exclaimed. "Has the date of the marriage been set? I sure want to be there."

"No, not yet, but of course I'll let you know. Will Charles be able to bring you up to us?"

"One never knows his schedule. I worry about him, too. He's been running around like a madman ever since Ann divorced him. She's a bit like Rosemary. She acts like our Lord Jesus has a telephone. That's not the way we were brought up."

Mother laughed and said, "It sure wasn't. It seems to me that it makes mockery of Christ to pass judgment on others all the time."

Aunt Lucy quoted from the Bible. "*Judge not, lest ye be judged.* Isn't that what Christ taught?"

"You're right, Aunt Lucy," I interjected, "and she's turned John into a Jesus Freak."

"Oh, Lord Jesus, help us!" Mother prayed.

What irony! I thought. Rosemary relied on her interpretation of Jesus's principles to condemn others, and we quoted the same principles to combat her. Poor Jesus! It must be difficult figuring out all these religious contradictions."

Chapter 4

The Conclusion

After arriving home from our weekend outing at our beloved Aunt Lucy's, we found two messages on our voice mail. One was from our minister, Mr. Miller. Typically, he chuckled before he hung up. His habit was well-known among our church congregation, and most people considered it a nervous problem. How many times it had been brought to his attention was not known, but he continued to emit the sound whether the matter was amusing or serious. At the end of his voice mail to us, he chuckled.

The other message was from Mrs. Shane, who invited our family for church and dinner the next Sunday. This was a disturbing call, and when Jim heard the news, he yelled adamantly, "I'm not going!" We all shared his feelings, but we knew that we would go to the vipers' den for John's sake. It seemed to be the family credo.

The next morning, Mother called Mr. Miller, and he agreed to join us for dinner in the middle of the week. He had stated at his last meeting with us that he would consider our situation and search for any way that he could contribute advice. Our entire family expressed the hope that he had found some means of helping us with our enigma. We could not have been more wrong.

Mother next called Mrs. Shane, who informed us that Rosemary and John had returned safely and that her daughter's foot was much better. She expressed delight that we could join their family the next weekend and said that John was staying with them in their guest room for a few days. We assumed that he was receiving more indoctrination and that anything productive Charles had said was now put out of John's mind by Rosemary. A feeling of resignation took over, and we did not discuss it any more that day. We were simply weary from the whole traumatic drama.

On Wednesday evening, Mr. Miller came. He chuckled and asked Father for a contribution for the church's summer school for young people. Father graciously agreed. When Father brought up the subject of his eldest son, Mr. Miller mentioned that he had given the matter considerable thought, but just could not figure out a means by which he could help us in our dilemma.

I decided that I would see if our minister had any views on the contemporary turmoil in the world. "Mr. Miller," I said, "I've become very interested in the radicalism of a minority in the Muslim faith. Most Muslims condemn the behavior of terrorists, but they do not seem capable of controlling them."

"Oh, it's dreadful," he exclaimed.

"Then shouldn't the Christian church start considering the oncoming menace?"

Mr. Miller seemed puzzled and asked, "Do you have something in mind?"

"Well, I've been reading a lot about it, and it seems to me that the Christian church needs to unify against this imposing force."

"What do you mean, *unify?*"

"The Eastern Orthodox Churches and Western Catholicism should become one, and our Protestantism and the Jewish faith should be included in some way."

Mr. Miller chuckled. "Oh, my, but you are asking a lot. How could we ever do that?"

"But the church is divided over rather foolish reasons. Are we just going to allow radical Muslims to run over us without doing anything?"

Mr. Miller chuckled. "Oh, they won't do that!"

I was perturbed. "Mr. Miller, in the statistics course I had at school, we studied how demographics show that Europe will be Muslim by the year 2050. Their growth rate is three times that of other religions."

Mr. Miller chuckled again, which aggravated me. Everyone else around the table seemed studiously focused on their plates, perhaps in an effort to avoid the discussion. I quickly decided to see if the minister knew the history of the church. I brought up some material from a recent course I had taken. "Mr. Miller, we know that our western Christian philosophy comes from the Greek reliance on mankind's reason, and that eastern Christian philosophy comes from a reliance on otherworldly spiritualism. Should not some compromise be made between the two in order to unify against the rise of the force against us?"

Again a chuckle escaped from Mr. Miller. "Oh, my, but you have studied the problem. I admire you for it, but I do not see any chance of unification or any compromise."

"So, we are just going to continue bickering about this and that while our world is being subjugated?"

"Oh, that's too severe," the minister replied with another chuckle.

"Really? When so much is at stake? Shouldn't Christians and Jews join together as a force against subjugation by a third religion?"

"Oh, Tom," Mr. Miller exclaimed. "Now you've gone too far. That could never happen."

"And why not?"

"Well . . ." Mr. Miller hesitated. "It just couldn't."

I guessed it was better to drop the subject; he clearly didn't understand me. So I said, "Well, it's just a theory that's going around." I dropped my tone as if we might as well change the subject.

"Tom," Father commented, "I've not heard you talk like that before. I know you've been studying philosophy at college, but has that given you an interest in Muslim radicalism?"

Mr. Miller joined in. "Yes, Tom, I've not heard you speak like that. I think it's most admirable that you are taking your studies so seriously."

His attitude aggravated me, so I said, "It seems to me, Mr. Miller, that our church is not giving much consideration to the advance of radicalism in the Muslim faith."

He did not chuckle, but smiled. "Oh, yes we are! I assure you that we think about it a lot."

I decided to force the issue. "And what does our Christian church plan to do about it?"

Mr. Miller looked rather vacant. There was an awkward silence.

Mother helped the struggling minister by changing the subject. She told Mr. Miller that we would be back at our farm again the next weekend.

He chuckled. "Oh, people come, and people go."

Mr. Miller did not stay long after dinner; but during the conversation in the family room about the Jesus Plan, he did quote an old axiom that we often mentioned afterward: Ignorance is the greatest power on earth. He stated that it causes wars, hatred, and crime. Other than that, he achieved the purpose of his visit—that was, collecting money for the youth summer program at the church. He left without giving us any advice.

John returned the next morning and told us how glad he was that we had accepted the invitation from the Shanes. To my parents he said, "Your understanding makes me very happy." To me, he delivered a well-rehearsed statement, which I am sure came from the vampire: "You are too inexperienced to fully appreciate the wonder of God's message to us through his Son, our Lord Jesus."

"Guess so!" I flippantly responded, thinking, *That evil bitch has been at him again. God help us!"*

"Don't worry, Tom," John continued. "You're still my brother, and I love you very much. I just pray that you will soon see the light shining from above."

I laughed. "Thanks, John, but I'm more worried about traffic lights down here right now, if you don't mind."

John shook his head. "You are always the joker! But you'll understand some day."

I could hardly stand it and practically barked back at him. "John, didn't you comprehend anything that our cousin Charles said to you? He tried to make you see how Rosemary is influencing you. He's really very concerned and thinks you've been brainwashed."

"Oh, Rosemary and I pray for him earnestly."

"Oh!" I moaned. "Give me a break!" Then I went out on the patio and sat down. I picked up a newspaper from the glass table and started reading the headlines.

John called out to me. "You'll understand someday."

I did not respond.

The next Sunday, Mother arranged for Jim to spend the day with his friend Joe so that he would avoid going with us to the Jesus Plan. The rest of us went with feelings of trepidation. I know I'd said that I would never go to another of the Reverend's sermons, but Mother persuaded me with her "for John's sake" line. We arrived in time for a blessing from the Reverend at the entrance of the shoddy building. He was very serious and put a hand on the top of each head as we walked into the church. I sort of slipped out from under it, and he gave me a look of displeasure. It did not break my heart.

On we went into the citadel of ignorance. Mrs. Shane was playing at the organ and continually looking around so that she could nod to people entering the sanctuary. Again, we did not recognize the music. I just sat there quietly. How could a Protestant church have such unusual songs? I'd been in various churches, but they all sang about the same thing. What was going on here?

We sat down near the organ and smiled at Mrs. Shane's recognition. She greeted us with a special blast from the heavenly bells that the organ was capable of producing. Finally the service started. Reverend Shane entered the pulpit from a back door and looked down at the audience. He slowly raised a hand with which to deliver a blessing. Then he uttered in his loud raspy voice,

"Halleluiah, my chosen ones!" The church members responded with an equally loud salutation, "Halleluiah, Reverend." I began squirming a bit.

"I shall read the gospel lesson for the day," the holy man proclaimed. "Let us heed the word of the Lord in Proverbs 20:1." He opened a very large Bible and read, "Wine is a mocker, intoxicating drink arouses brawling, and whomever is led astray by it is not wise."

At that point I was confused. Why did he use a quote from the Old Testament? Jesus was only in the New Testament. However, it seemed I was getting ahead of the Reverend's quotes. He turned next to the New Testament to read from John, chapter two.

"On the third day there was a wedding in Cana of Galilee, and the Mother of Jesus was there. And both Jesus was called, and his disciples, to the marriage. And when they wanted wine, the Mother of Jesus saith unto him, 'They have no wine.' Jesus saith unto them, 'Fill the waterpots with water.' And they filled them up to the brim. And he saith unto them, 'Draw out now, and bear unto the governor of the feast.' And they bare it, and the ruler of the feast tasted the water that was made wine."

Later I found out that the Reverend only used phrases from the actual quote, but he stated his message quickly. Huffed up and standing very straight, the Reverend said, "There are some who believe that Jesus made real wine, but are we to believe that His Holiness would indulge in making or drinking something that the Bible itself preaches against? Just look at the two quotes I have given you. The first is the warning, the second shows that Christ made a grape drink that was not fermented into wine."

I squirmed. *He's crazy!* I thought. *There's nothing in those two quotes that mentions a grape drink. Christ made wine; we learned that from the cradle up!* I wanted to leave, but that was impossible. I whispered to Mother, "He's wrong!" but she did not respond.

The sermon continued for an hour and a half. I was almost asleep several times, but Father nudged me. Then there was the communion, followed by the collection plate. When the entire service was finally over, I whispered to Father, "Is there a back door?" He shook his head and whispered, "Bear up for John's sake!"

God, I thought. *What a person has to do for a brother these days!*

After the service, John and Rosemary came through the audience to us. She was so sweet and loving, it almost made me ill. Her foot had healed, and she was all heavenly graces as she greeted people and introduced our family. When I found out there was a restroom in the basement, I excused myself and left. Anything would have been better than hearing her exude her sugary venom.

At last we were at the dinner table in the Shane's humble home, a wooden structure sparsely furnished, except for the many pictures of Christ throughout the place. After the blessing, which rambled on at least ten minutes, we started passing the "vitals," as Mrs. Shane described her various dishes. The word "grub" would have been better, as it seemed that her courses could have been listed in a Southern cookbook: fried chicken, sauerkraut, squash, grits, and sweet potatoes. Yet I must be kind; she had seasoned them well. It was the dessert that had some room for improvement. Her bread pudding was just not up to snuff, but no one said anything negative. We wanted very much to make a fine impression, and we did—as far as the food was concerned. Again, it was the conversation that cast a pall over the get-together.

Father thanked the Reverend for the service in the church, and Mother added her appreciation. I could not lie and dared to suggest that many think that Jesus did drink wine. "Oh, that blessed man would not do that!" Rosemary immediately attacked. Then she added, "Oh, Lord God, forgive him!"

Reverend Shane nodded and said quite loudly, "Amen!"

I did not want an argument, but I asked, "Does it matter whether Christ drank wine or water?"

"Oh, it does," Mrs. Shane commented and looked at her daughter. "It does, doesn't it dear."

"It most certainly does," the viper continued. "You heard my Father's blessed sermon this morning. He pointed out that Christ would never do anything that contradicted the Bible's laws."

I'll be up to my neck in crap if I carry on with this!" I backed off and said, "I just wondered."

"Well, your wonderings sometimes mislead you, my son," the Reverend said. "I've been watching you. You seem to live up to your name. You like to doubt things—even biblical truths."

"Guess I'm just cursed by my name," I responded, trying to add a little humor.

"Oh! Don't say that!" Rosemary interjected. "You must never think of yourself as cursed. The devil is always waiting for a victim. If you admit weakness, that horrible monster will step in quickly and take advantage of you. God, forgive him."

I should not have brought up the next thing I mentioned, but I did. "Is the devil around as much as one's angel?"

"They are both with us always!" the Reverend announced in his ceremonial tone. "That's why we must always be on guard. My daughter is correct. You must be more careful."

'Yes," Mrs. Shane repeated. "One must be very careful. Evil is always around."

I decided that I would leave well enough alone. "Thank you!" I said, trying to sound sincere. However, I did not fool the vampire, who gave me a look that would scare demons in hellfire.

After the dinner we were invited into a salon full of large, over-stuffed chairs. We settled down for a conversation about the forthcoming wedding.

"Have you set a date?" Mother asked.

"Not yet," Rosemary answered sweetly.

John reported in. "We'll be up to see you some time soon and discuss our plans for the wedding."

"Oh, that will be wonderful," Mother responded. "Be sure and let me know what I can do."

Mrs. Shane said, "We don't want to bother you, although I'm sure you would do whatever you can. Rosemary and I are working out details. One thing you can do is to send us a list of your family and friends that you wish to invite."

"Thank you, dear," Mother answered.

And so the conversation continued for some time. Nothing was really decided, and no definite details were explained. I thought it was an exercise about nothing.

As usual, the families did not blend well together. By the time we departed, I realized that I would never be invited back to their den, but that only gave me comfort.

The next day John came home for some of his personal things. He said that he had left most of his things at home because his room at the Shanes was small. Mother helped him for a while, and then she decided that she should make one last attempt to save her son. She asked him for a short chat, and they went into the family room. I was working on a computer in a niche in the family room and could hear them talking.

"John," Mother said as they sat down on the couch out of sight from me, "you are so young. But the main thing has to do with your livelihood. What are you and Rosemary going to live on?"

"I'm working for the Jesus Plan," he replied earnestly.

"But surely that's no job that would support a family. You do want children, don't you?"

"Of course!"

"Are you sure that Rosemary can bear children?"

"Why shouldn't she?"

"Dear boy, she seems very sickly. Her Mother told me that she's often ill. And remember how easily she hurt herself on the walk in the park."

"Anyone can fall. No, she's fine."

Mother hesitated and then asked, "Well, what about expenses?"

"My salary will be enough at first."

"Of course, but as I said, how can you make enough to support a family? John, I want you to go to college."

"Mother, I'm not like Tom. He's always been a good student."

"But you can be too," she responded. "You just spent too much time in athletics. If you really applied yourself to your studies, I'm sure you could prepare yourself for a career."

"No, Mother! You see, Rosemary wants us to settle down. I won't need a college education. We'll both work at the Jesus Plan at first, and that will be enough for a while."

After a few moments of silence, Mother said, "John, I have a wonderful idea. I'll sell part of my farm and buy you both a trailer that you can put in a trailer park near the university. She can work while you go to school. Many young couples are doing this. After all, you have GI Bill. Why not take advantage of it?"

John was silent. Finally he said, "Would you really do that, Mother? You'd sell part of the farm you love?"

"For my beloved son, I'd do anything."

John was silent and then said, "I'll talk with Rosemary about it."

"Oh, John, my darling boy, you've made me so happy."

I am sure she threw her arms around him and gave him a hug. They stood up and noticed me in the far corner. Mother said, "Did you hear us, Tom? John is going to college too!"

When I opened my mouth for an answer, John hurriedly said, "Well, we shall see."

I tried to be encouraging and said, "Gee, John, that's great news!

Mother left the room to tell her husband about the plan.

John came over by me. "Tom, I've been wanting a little chat with you. Do you have time?"

"Of course," I replied and walked with him over by the fireplace mantel. We sat in our parents' fireside chairs. "I'm glad you're going to use your GI Bill. It seems silly not to use it."

"We'll see," he responded, "but that's not what I want to talk with you about. I want you to be honest with me, brother to brother."

I nodded.

"Tell me, do you like Rosemary? Be honest!"

Shaking my head, I let go with what had been bothering me. "John, I don't care for her. She's very pretty, but there's just something strange about her. Also, I don't like the way she dominates you."

"She doesn't dominate me," he said, looking surprised.

"John, if you marry her, you'll never have a life of your own. You'll only be her slave."

He laughed. "Tom, that's ridiculous."

"No, it isn't. She has some power over you. I don't know how to express it, but when I watch you with her, you seem like another person—one that I don't even know!"

"Tom, that can't be true. Besides, she likes you very much."

Slowly shaking my head, I replied, "John, she loathes me, but you can't see it. She knows the way I feel, and I'm sure she's trying to turn you against me."

John was silent. I knew I had hit on a delicate matter. After a few seconds, John tried a rebuttal. "No, that's not true, but she does wish that our family was more in line with the Jesus Plan. You see, the church we attended all our lives really didn't give us much."

"With that, I definitely agree. I've decided that our minister is a half-educated loon, but Rosemary goes too far in the opposite direction. She's a complete ignoramus in my opinion."

"Tom," my brother exclaimed, "she's far better educated than I am." I shook my head as he continued. "Rosemary wants to spread Christ's love to everyone. She's practically a saint."

"John, her interpretation of Christ is a cover for her ignorance. I'm sorry to be so blunt, but that's the way I see it."

"Don't you believe in Lord Jesus anymore?" His face showed that he was greatly troubled.

"I want to, John, but I'm beginning to think that the Arabs have understood Him better than the Christians. Mohammed took Christ's message to heart and placed it in the Koran. He made a great prophet of Christ, not a divine human being like we do."

Still concerned, John asked, "You don't believe in the divinity of Christ?"

"John, if I believe the Christmas story, don't I also have to believe that Moses brought down three-hundred-pound tablets from heaven, that Mohammed flew off to paradise, and that Lord Krishna had a hundred avatars? Who's right in the religious bubble?"

John looked at the floor. "Tom, you've confused me. I can't argue with you. You see things on such a broad scale. I think I prefer the security of Christ's love, and that's enough."

"I agree. I think we've said enough. You say she likes me. I don't think so, but I'm willing to like her for your sake."

"Thanks, Tom." He smiled and we parted.

The next day John requested a meeting with Mother and Father. I asked if I could join in. He was not sure that he wanted me involved but finally relented. He had talked with Rosemary and wanted to explain their feelings about Mother's proposition. After everyone was seated in the family room, John began his astounding, but not unexpected news.

"Rosemary did not like the proposition you made, Mother, about buying us a trailer. As I told you, she would prefer that we remain in the Jesus Plan and have a much simpler life. The vagaries of this world have no attraction for her. She just wants us to be happy."

Mother and Father were both taken aback by his revelation. "What do you mean by vagaries?" Mother asked.

"You know, things that are not important."

"What is not important?" she continued.

"Well, a university education is unpredictable. Our church can give us a happiness that would be destroyed by education."

Father spoke up. "I've never heard anything so ridiculous. An education is the only thing worth having."

"It's true, my dear," Mother commented. "Look at your Father and me. We did not have the benefit of a higher education, and we've stayed small. If I didn't have an income from my farm, we would not have the lifestyle that we have."

"But Mother, you are happy people. Chances are that an education would have made you miserable."

Father asked, "Whom do you know who is miserable because they received an education?"

"Why, Tom here is a perfect example."

I laughed. "Why do you think I'm miserable?"

"Look at the confusion in your mind. Yesterday you could not tell the difference between Moses, Mohammed, and Christ!"

"Good God!" I exclaimed, "Well, if that's what you got out of our conversation, I must not have been explaining myself very well."

Mother also protested. "John, your brother is enjoying college very much. It's wonderful that he chose Lake Forest College, because he can live here at home. I think it's making him very responsible and content. He's hardly miserable."

"Rosemary does not want me to enter the university. She feels that I would be much happier if I didn't clog up my mind with the diversions of this world."

"What diversions?" Father asked.

"Oh, things that take one away from the Jesus Plan—like history and science."

I shook my head. "John, surely you are kidding?"

"No, I'm not. Rosemary feels we will be better off in our own environment . . . that is, in the church. We don't need extraneous knowledge."

Mother and Father looked at me as if they were helpless. Then John added to their befuddlement.

"Rosemary thought it would be fine if you, Mother, did sell part of your farm and bought us a house near the church."

Mother was speechless.

"You can't expect us to do that, John," said Father. "How could you support a new home when you have no means of income?"

"I'm working at the Jesus Plan!"

"What kind of a future is that?" Father asked.

Mother had made up her mind, and I was proud of her. "No, John. I cannot do what you ask. Our farm is the basis for our livelihood. How can you expect us to buy you a house?"

"You were going to buy a trailer!"

"That's hardly a house. Besides, I assumed you would pay me back for the trailer when you finished school. But a house? That's too expensive. And how could you afford to maintain it?"

"Rosemary will be very disappointed."

Mother looked askance. "I'm very sorry, but it's just out of the question."

Father helped the situation. "Your Mother and I are planning to give you a new car for your wedding present. And there will naturally be some other things."

"Yes," Mother piped in. "Your silver service!"

"Thanks, folks, but I must talk with Rosemary first. I'll call her and tell her I'm coming down there this evening." He went into the entrance hall and called his fiancée. Suddenly we heard him raise his voice with a frightful tone. He returned and said, "Rosemary's ill. I have to go immediately. She wasn't feeling well this morning, but I didn't want to mention it. Now it appears that she's much worse, and they are even thinking of taking her to a hospital. I'll call you when I know what the situation is."

We saw him off with words of sympathy. As he drove out of our driveway, my mind dwelled on the vampire. *If only she would kick the bucket.* Later that evening, John called from the local St. Agnes Hospital. Rosemary was being operated on. Mother, Father, and I left quickly to be with him. Jim stayed home, working over his homework.

After assuring the hospital receptionist that we were relatives, we were permitted entrance into the surgical section. John was sitting in a waiting room. I was glad that the Reverend was not there, but John said that the Shanes were on their way. John explained that Rosemary had problems with her digestion and that she had been quite ill that morning. Her retching and coughing had lasted a long time. However, she suddenly felt better and told John he should go home and not worry.

During the afternoon, she had become worse. The Reverend and Mrs. Shane prayed over her for some time, but when Rosemary was bent over from the terrible pain, they decided that she needed medical help. They carefully placed her aching body in their car and drove to the emergency ward of St. Agnes Hospital.

Suffering excruciating pain, Rosemary had passed out while waiting for a doctor. The nurse attending her room immediately called for help, and two doctors rushed to the bedside. After receiving stimulants, Rosemary was aroused but was still enduring considerable pain. They took X-rays and made a rather startling discovery: Her innards did not seem to be in the correct locations. When I heard that, an idea came to me. *What would you expect in a vampire?* But I suppose I should not have been so facetious when someone was so ill.

Then the great healer himself came with Mrs. Shane. The Reverend asked where the operating room was located, but they told him he was not allowed there during a procedure. He stated that he only wanted to bless the room and could do it from the outside. A nurse led him down the hall, and I watched as he stopped in front of the double doors and began his harangue.

Since he was praying in a rather loud tone, a nurse opened the door and looked out at one point, evidently checking on what the raucous was about. The red light above the door had gone off when it was opened, but the nurse quickly closed the door. Evidently she locked it again, because the Reverend couldn't open it when he tried. Finally he finished and came back to the waiting room.

Meanwhile, Mrs. Shane had already blessed the entire hospital, so the two of them had time for us. They greeted us kindly, and we all sat down for the wait. After an hour, the Reverend asked a nurse if she could check on how the operation was going; but she refused, saying, "No one is allowed in the surgical room when the red light is on." So we nervously waited two more hours. Fortunately, everyone was tired, and there was no conversation.

At last the door opened and a doctor came in. We all stood up and listened. He explained that Rosemary was fine, but the operation had taken a long time because of the unusual situation that was discovered once they had opened her lower stomach area. Her appendix had grown to an unnatural length and had intertwined with her other organs. It had required the removal of the extended appendix and the placement of the other organs in their natural order. Such a problem was rare but was easily taken care of.

"Can she still have children?" asked Mrs. Shane.

The doctor hesitated. "Probably," he said. "There are so many things that can be done today for childbirth. I wouldn't worry about that now."

"When can I see her?" asked the Reverend. "I would like to offer some prayers over her."

"You are a minister?" the doctor asked.

The Reverend bowed most sanctimoniously.

"She will be in the post-operative ward until she revives," the doctor explained. "Then she will be assigned a room. Once she is there, the nurse will take you to see her."

"I'd like to pray over her in the post-operative ward," the Reverend said. "That is when she needs prayer the most."

The doctor almost laughed but quickly pulled out a handkerchief and pretended to sneeze. "I'm sorry, but the hospital administration does not allow any visitors. You see, there are other patients in that room, and the danger of infection is very great."

The Reverend nodded his head most majestically, but before he could say anything, the doctor left.

John then told us and the Shanes that we should leave. Rosemary might not revive for some time, and there was no need for us to wait. As we left, we expressed our sorrow that Rosemary was so ill. The Shanes embraced us but remained, because they had their prayer duties to perform.

Driving home, Mother said, "Oh, I'm so afraid that she won't be able to have children. Did you notice how the doctor hesitated before he answered Mrs. Shane's question about childbirth?"

Pity the child that would be reared by that woman! I thought.

"It is a worrisome problem," Father said. "It did not sound good. Wonder what made her appendix wind through her intestines like that?"

Well, snakes do crawl! I said to myself.

Mother and Father both discussed all sorts of possibilities for Rosemary's problem, but their major concern was the fear that she was now not capable of bearing children. It seemed to be one more reason for stopping the marriage, and they decided they should talk with John. I did not think it necessary. He was already steadfast in the Jesus Plan, and I was sure that the Shanes would call Rosemary's recovery a miracle from God.

When the ailing fiancée awakened and was ready for transport to a room, she insisted that it be private. John agreed, of course, even though it used all the money that he had saved in the army. Our parents thought her selfishness was another point they could use in preventing the marriage. Of course they were wrong.

Then an incident occurred that was to hinder any thought of calling off the marriage. Mother was walking by a florist shop and noticed a large porcelain vase in the shape of a beautiful Persian cat. She thought it was very beautiful and had it filled with flowers and sent to Rosemary at the hospital."

John came home the afternoon of the vampire's third day in the private room, and I heard him ask Mother, "Why did you do something so hurtful?"

Dumbstruck, Mother stood and stared at her son. What on earth had she done that would cause such an accusation.

"You sent that cat to Rosemary to tell her that she was catty."

Mother sat down and started crying. It was pathetic. Suddenly all the fears and anxieties that had been building up in her mind and causing her sleeplessness and worry were released and expressed themselves in her flowing tears. She could not cease bawling.

John finally said, "Mother, I'm sorry. I know that can't be true. Rosemary was wrong to even think it. I know you couldn't be mean like that." He put his hands on her shoulders and tried to hug her. She cried even more, and he apologized again and again.

At last Mother found control of herself and weakly said, "Of course, I didn't think that. How could she even think so?"

"It's her nerves, Mother," John said in defense of his fiancée. "I'm sure she didn't mean it. She's just not herself after what she's been through."

Mother went on the offensive. "John, look at what we've been through. Our dearest son is marrying someone who has had a most negative influence on him. You would have never thought such a thing if she had not made it up. Your reasoning has been affected. You're not the sweet, kind, loving son that I've always admired. She's made you narrow and prejudiced through her so-called Jesus Plan."

"No, Mother!" John said in rebuttal.

"Yes," she continued. "And now we know that she will probably never have children. You'll be an old man alone, and you'll be doubly sorry." She started crying again.

John stood by her without words. How could he express his feelings when he knew that what she had said was true. After a short silence, he said that he had better return to the hospital.

"And one last thing before you go," Mother said, looking up at her son. "Why did she have to have a private room when she knew that you cannot afford it? Is she going to be so selfish all your lives? Oh, John, wake up to what you're doing. She's not for you. Stop before it's too late, I beg of you."

Mother stood up and looked at John. He was silent for a few seconds; then he hugged her and said, without replying to her outburst, "I have to go now. I'll stay at the Shane's again for a couple of days and see you later."

"Good-bye, my darling," she said and sat down, wiping her tears.

Life in our home slowly calmed down. Father kept himself busy painting one of his commissions. Jim and his friend Joe spent their time swimming, surfing on the Internet, and going to movies. I was busily using Google daily in my efforts to understand some philosophical problems I had encountered in my arguments with the Shanes. Mother continued her charity work through the church and often brought home news about the minister's chuckle. The family had definitely given up. John was going to marry the viper no matter what we said or did.

John informed us daily by phone about Rosemary's recovery. She was walking around the garden at the Shane's after four days in the hospital. Her recovery seemed complete. Finally, John called and told us that Rosemary and he were planning a visit with us. Mother invited them for dinner the next day, and he accepted. Again she asked that we not talk about religious matters or embarrass John with more efforts at changing his mind about the forthcoming marriage. The instructions were pointless. What else was there to discuss with them?

While waiting for the arrival of the vampire and my brother, the family was sitting in their usual places near the fireplace mantel. Suddenly Mother said, "I feel a strange cool draft. Does anyone else?"

"Yes, I do," Father replied. "Maybe I should make a fire. It was so warm today, I didn't think of it."

"I think it's a warning that the monster has arrived!" said Jim.

Mother rebuked him and said to Father, "Do make a fire. It just feels uncomfortable all of a sudden."

I was amused. "I agree with Jim," I said. "An evil spirit has flown in among us."

Jim laughed. "Perhaps it's John's angel."

"Jim!" Mother exclaimed. "You should be ashamed. Many people feel that they have a guardian angel."

"Yeah," he answered, "but John's has big frothy feathers. You can always feel that kind when they fly in."

Father laughed and Mother smiled, even while shaking her head. She pointed a finger at Jim and said, "Remember what I said! No religion or marriage in the conversation this evening."

Father had a fire burning when Rosemary and John came into the family room. She greeted everyone with her hands folded in prayer. After a few seconds, she looked up and said, "Thank you for your concern during my illness."

"Oh, my dear," Mother said, "motioning for her to sit on the couch, "we were so sorry for you."

"You need not have worried. I was in God's hands."

"Of course you were," Mother responded.

John joined his fiancée on the couch and said, "We have wonderful news. We've set the date for our marriage."

Father and Mother both proclaimed their pleasure. I frankly think that they were glad that the turmoil we had been living through was finally coming to an end. It was not the conclusion they would have wanted, but it was calming to know that it soon would end.

"It's to be May fifteenth."

"In so few weeks?" Mother gasped, quite surprised.

"Yes," Rosemary replied. "We saw no reason for delay."

No one responded, so Rosemary continued. "I know that you feel that we should probably wait a while, but we have solved our major problems."

"Yes," John said. "Reverend Shane has a disciple in the Jesus Plan who has come forward to help us."

"In what way?" Father asked.

"He has offered us a small house that he owns near the church. Our rent will be minimal, and he'll consider it a down payment for the time we can buy it."

"Oh, my goodness!" Mother cried out. "How wonderful!"

Bet the Reverend threatened that guy with hellfire to get it, I thought. *Sort of like a Catholic indulgence payment.*

Rosemary then said to Mother, "I know that you are afraid I can't bear children. Well, I can. My doctor has assured me of it."

Mother was about to express her joy, but Rosemary continued without letting her speak.

"I also want to inform all of you that I know you are against our marriage. You have made it quite obvious. You have insisted that John enter the university when he is not so inclined. You have offered money for a trailer but have refused to use it for a house. You have humiliated my parents and us by not accepting our way of life. You have demeaned John's guardian angel with wayward comments, and you have not been reverent when the Reverend and I have blessed you and yours. You see, you are not in the Jesus Plan and could therefore not possibly understand the way we have devoted ourselves to His service."

"But Rosemary," Mother finally interjected, "we want only the best for you. Surely you understand that."

"We do, Mother," John responded, but Rosemary gave him a look of dissatisfaction. He then added, "But we are depressed by what we have had to endure."

"What, for instance?" Father asked.

Rosemary's eyes glistened as she answered, "Rudeness, shallowness, and snide remarks, just to name a few of the humiliations!"

The family was speechless. Mother tried to appeal. "Oh, my dear, we certainly did not mean any harm."

The vampire rose. "We have to leave now," she said. John stood beside her, and they started out of the room. We had all stood up and were watching them go when the Evil Eye turned on us. The vampire stopped and said, "My mother will be in touch with you about our wedding plans."

"Thank you," said Mother.

The family watched as John and Rosemary drove out of the yard. Then we looked at each other in dismay.

Jim, who had been sitting quietly, said, "She hates us!"

"Loathes us, for sure," I added.

"Oh, God," Mother said tearfully, "what is happening to our happy family?"

"Her version of Christ is worse than the vengeful God of the Old Testament," Father said. "He had mercy; she doesn't."

We felt as if a whirlwind had blown through, and we were suddenly lost in its turmoil. We had lost a son and brother, and our happy home would never be the same.

Chapter 5

The Wedding

Weddings always bring together strangers who have little in common and who will probably never see each other again. Never was it so true as on that beautiful day in May when the vampire put her teeth into my brother.

Since it was traditional for assembled guests at a wedding to be divided between the bride's and groom's relatives and friends, Mother was allowed more spaces than she had anticipated. She first thought of Aunt Lucy and Charles. She just hoped that the latter would not bring one of his trollops. There was always the possibility that his ex-wife would come with their daughters if he invited them, but since they lived in Florida and did not keep in touch with our family, chances were that they would not attend. Mother did not want any arguments or conflicts at such a time. While there were only those two close relatives, they were enough dynamite for an explosion. Murphy's law persisted: If it can happen, it will. And it did.

Then there were the friends that needed consideration. First, of course, was the minister Mr. Miller. Fortunately, he was not conducting the ceremony. Mother did not want any chuckles accompanying the question of "Who has the ring?" or "Is there anyone here who has objections to this union." She was afraid a chuckle after the latter would bring unwanted catcalls from certain relatives. She wanted a peaceful, pleasant ceremony and carefully selected the friends who would attend. Neighbors and members of various organizations took most of the invitations. When she finished, Mother was quite satisfied with her selection. The troublesome Charles was her major concern.

Gifts began arriving soon after the invitations were sent out. Aunt Lucy sent a handmade blanket with a beautiful design that used all the rainbow colors. She must have worked on it for a long time in hopes of being able to give it to someone on a special occasion. While some people consider such a gift a bit gauche, Mother was delighted. Rosemary, however, found it rather odd that there was no religious message involved in the design. Her conclusion was, "Well, we can use it for something." When I heard what she said about the blanket, I did have an idea. *Yeah, like suffocating yourself!*

Then there was the questionable statue from Charles. It was carved marble, but somewhat obsequious. If observed at a distance, it seemed simply a play of forms. Yet up close, one could possibly discern a suggestive entanglement of human bodies. Mother was not sure that it was appropriate. The vampire did not understand it at first, but upon close examination, she quickly declared it insulting and asked that it be returned to Charles. Such a thing had never been done before, but John took on the obligation, saying, "I'll see that he gets it." I knew where I would have liked to put it!

Most neighbors and friends contributed pieces from the silver service that Rosemary registered at an expensive jewelry store downtown. The pattern the vampire selected showed a complete lack of taste as far as I was concerned. It was so simple it could have been from Walmart. However, while Mother and Father agreed with me for a change, they completed the set as part of their gift.

There were some changes to the traditional run of affairs at a wedding. For instance, there was to be no bachelor party for John the evening before the ceremony that I called "the execution." Instead of the groom participating in a raucous binge with drunkards and wastrels, there was to be a prayer service in the Jesus Plan. Charles protested when he heard about that aspect of the wedding plans, but his complaint only pleased the vampire. I heard her say to John in the sweetest voice this side of heaven, "John, you can go to such a demeaning event with a group of rowdy men if you wish, but you'll have to make that choice." Of course he did not go.

Another change that I found absolutely ridiculous had to do with the music of the ceremony. Brides for ages have entered the church to the Wedding March from Wagner's *Tannhauser* and then exited after the service to the music of Mendelssohn. When a member of the church asked the vampire why the time-honored music had been changed, Rosemary answered in tones that would have made the screech-owl Lilith shudder, "Those foreigners' music will not be played at my wedding!" So, of course, they were not used. She would enter the church to "Jesus Walks with Me!" and then exit to "Saved at Last, Saved at Last." Where she found such oddities, no one knew, but I thought they fit in perfectly with all the mish-mash that she had made of the ceremony. Our family did not look forward to the blessed day.

There was also the passing back and forth of anything but compliments when the matter of the wedding apparel was discussed. When Mother asked Mrs. Shane if she could help her and Rosemary choose a lovely bride's dress, she was quickly informed that no help was needed. Besides, Mrs. Shane was making the dress. That was quite a surprise. Mother said, wanting to be cordial, "My goodness, you are talented, Mrs. Shane. I never knew that you were such a seamstress."

"I'm already working on it," she replied.

Mother unfortunately exclaimed, "Oh, I do hope it will have a hoop skirt. I think Rosemary would be so beautiful as a southern girl."

Mrs. Shane answered using a word that we were sure she did not know the meaning of. "No, she would not want something so mundane."

"Oh, I've always loved hoop skirts. I wanted one for my wedding, but they were just too expensive."

"That's what I mean," Mrs. Shane said. "We did not think we should waste money on such a frivolous thing, especially since I can make the dress myself."

Mother made one last attempt at contributing to the bride's apparel. She said, "Well, if you don't need me for the dress, I wonder if you would let me contribute to Rosemary's trousseau?"

Mrs. Shane hesitated and then replied, "Oh, I think flowers are a personal matter. You might pick something she doesn't like—calla lilies, for instance. Let's let her choose the flowers."

Mother gave up trying to be useful. She told me that she would not make any more suggestions for anything pertaining to the wedding. It was a pity that her insights and knowledge were not heeded, because the dress that appeared at the wedding was talked about long after the affair—and not in kind terms.

John did ask Mother if she would look at the jacket that Rosemary had decorated for his apparel at the wedding. She agreed, but when he took it out of his clothes bag, she was startled. So was I. It was a white jacket with gold braid trim. Unfortunately, the gold was hanging in places that were not apropos. The coat looked more like a pastiche than a formal wedding jacket. "John, dear," said Mother, "this looks a little like something a clown might wear at the circus. I don't mean to say that it is not well-decorated because it is. It's just that I think it's a bit overdone for such an occasion."

"What would you suggest?" John asked.

"Well, you see these long streamers of braid from each shoulder? They detract from the line—that is, the shape—of the coat and seem out of place."

"What else?"

"Well, the angle at which the braid is attached to the front of the jacket makes it appear more like a child's toy. It destroys the solemnity of the occasion."

"Oh, Mother," John commented, "I don't know if we should change it. Rosemary did it herself, and she has excellent taste. She's assured me of that."

Mother bit her lip and stepped back. She reexamined the coat, but after a few moments of reflection, she shook her head. She had decided that she should not change the decoration because of the consequences her action might provoke. She simply said, "Well, John, you're going to be wearing it. If you feel comfortable in it, then let it stay as it is. Rosemary has spent a lot of time on it, so if you're pleased, why not let it be?"

John gave Mother a hug. "I'm so glad you like it. She'll be very pleased."

Our family was given little chance to participate in the wedding plans. The Shanes were in control of everything. It is, of course, traditional for the bride's family to be in charge of a daughter's wedding, but the way the Shanes handled it seemed improper. There were certain things that our family would have liked to know, but any inquiries we made were always rebuffed. The usual reply was, "That's being done according to the Jesus Plan." Since we never really understood the so-called plan and had no means by which we could learn more about it, we just simply had to wait and accept what crumbs the Shanes would pass on to us.

One thing only was certain. The date of the marriage was May 15. As it approached, Mother and Father became quite tense. The arrival of Aunt Lucy and Charles the day before the event did not help settle my parents' nerves. In fact, their being quite uninformed about wedding details only made our guests more inquisitive. Charles finally said, "What in the hell is going on around here? You haven't been included in anything!" Father explained the situation several times, but his insights into the cause of the estrangement only added to the confusion.

Yet there was no way of quieting Charles. He called John and asked if he could have a drink with him that evening. When John said that he no longer drank, Charles yelled into the phone, "What in the hell is wrong with you, John? Are you going to let that hellion rule you the rest of your life? You'd better stand up to her now, or you're lost forever. And as far as the Jesus Plan, you can stick it up your ass." He then banged the receiver down on the phone. I laughed. That evening John did not come home, and our family seemed ready more for a wake than a wedding. Neither Aunt Lucy's charm nor Charles' wit could cheer us up.

As I mentioned earlier, May 15 was a beautiful day. Spring flowers were in bloom, birds were chirping in the trees, and the sun promised warmth. The wedding was scheduled for two o'clock, followed by a reception and then a dinner by invitation. John came home while the family was having breakfast. He was dressed in the regalia created by Rosemary. Leave it to Charles to say it: "John, you look like a Walt Disney creation."

Aunt Lucy bawled Charles out. "Dear boy," she said to John, "don't pay any attention to that ape. You just look resplendent."

John thanked her and said to Charles, "If you don't like it, you don't have to stay, you know."

"Oh, ho, ho!" Charles exclaimed, raising his voice on the last syllable. "She's injected her poison in him!"

John raised a fist. "One more remark like that, and you'll get it."

Charles waved a hand as if what he had said was nothing. "John, relax," he suggested. "You're just a bit uptight with the whole affair. I'll never forget my first wedding. I felt numb most of the day."

"And drunk ever since," Jim said, and everyone laughed, including Charles.

Mother brought John some breakfast, and he pulled a chair to the table by Aunt Lucy. She began telling him about some of the activities taking place at the farm. It was the pattern for all conversation that took place before leaving for the wedding. John looked very pompous in his outfit while sitting among the family in their housecoats. Yet nobody tried making jokes about it. Everyone was careful to avoid any comment that might upset the garishly dressed groom. John left early, because the Jesus Plan had a prayer meeting before the nuptials. He invited the family, but we refused.

As her son drove out of the yard, Mother began crying. Aunt Lucy tried comforting her, but it was to no avail. Mother's heart was tearing in half. She could not accept what was happening. She sat crying and grieving. "He's making such a horrible mistake. He'll never have children. She'll dominate him all his life, and he'll never be with us again. Our family is falling apart!" Then she began bawling. It was truly pathetic. No one could say anything that gave her relief. She was miserable. Soon her eyes were red and swollen, and she was walking around bent over. But she could not cease crying. It cast a gloom over all of us.

Time demanded that we depart for the Jesus Plan. Jim rode with Aunt Lucy and Charles. Father and I took care of Mother, seating her in the car and listening to her sobs all the way to the church. Once there she calmed down enough for the entrance into the citadel.

An usher with small waxy wings pinned on his back led us to the front of the building. We could not help but be amused by the flopping of the attached wings. Even Mother muffled a laugh. "It's so absurd," Charles whispered. Yet after we saw what was ahead, we realized that the usher must have been a lower echelon angel. The small choir also had wings, and the organist, our dear Mrs. Shane, had reached the archangel level with large feathered ones. Charles could hardly control himself. I was having the same problem, especially when I looked across the aisle and saw wings on several members of the bride's guests. The place was beginning to look like an angel hoedown.

Gradually the church filled up with guests. On the groom's side, there was an occasional laugh when someone was amused at what seemed a gathering of the Valkyries. On the bride's side, a serious mood prevailed, with many of the guests holding their hands in prayer. Charles whispered to me, "It's like a preview of hell and heaven!" I nodded and thought, *Dear God, what a sacrilege these people make of Christ's message of peace and goodwill toward men!*

At that moment a loud burst from the organ opened the Heavenly Throne. A door covered with paper roses opened, and the Reverend entered; but he was not at all as we expected. There were no wings or anything frivolous. Instead, a vengeful, solemn preacher of the Lord came slowly forward. His rough face and beacon-like eyes caused consternation. He protracted a very serious mood. When he reached the pulpit and gazed at the guests, it was so unpleasant, one would have thought his purpose for being there was to threaten us, not to perform a wedding ceremony. He then asked in grave tones for us to stand for prayer. We did.

His long prayer unfolded with all the characteristics of the abysmally ignorant. Hellfire and the castigation of sins were simply not topics suitable for a wedding, but he was evidently adamant about carrying out the Jesus Plan approach to everything. His harangue lasted an inappropriate amount of time, and when he finished with "Amen!" the organ again let out a loud peal of joyous music. I think it was from Handel's *Messiah*, but I am not sure. The music abruptly changed, and "Jesus Walk with Me" flowed through the air. The audience started turning for a look at the back. Either the bride or the Virgin Mary was entering.

Rosemary was not dressed at all in the manner we expected. Her long white dress was quite simple, and she had not yet earned wings. Yet she was ghastly beautiful. Her large eyes shone like beacons, and her dark hair was a mass of curls around her powdered face. I had never seen such a bride. She was not the celestial figure I had expected, but more of an aesthetic alien, something unseen before on the terrestrial plane. The thick white powder on her face highlighted the darkness of her eyes.

It was a little unnerving as she walked up the aisle by herself, carrying a bouquet of carnations, each of which had a Bible quote attached to its stem. I thought I felt a cool chill in the air, yet the room was warm. I actually felt a shudder as the spectacle passed by. Charles whispered to me, "Are we in a witches' hovel or a church?" I shook my head. I had no answer. Then it dawned on me that there had not been any bridesmaids. How typical of Rosemary. It had to be her show.

While everyone was concentrating on the phenomenon that walked through the church, John, dressed in his celestial bandleader outfit, had suddenly appeared at the front of the building. He too looked rather serious as he watched his bride approach. *You should have had me as your groom beside you, John.* I thought. *Guess the great J-plan didn't allow it.* When Rosemary reached him, he turned sideways and stood beside her. They were ready for the ceremony.

The Jesus Plan's version of a wedding service was not that far removed from the traditional one. The greatest difference I noticed was that there was no ring-bearer. John merely pulled one out of his pocket. However, there was one very disturbing occurrence. When the reverend asked the fatal question about any grievances against the uniting of the couple, a sob resounded through the building. Unfortunately, Mother had succumbed to tears and unintentionally made the noise when she was wiping her nose. Rosemary never forgave her and added the incident to her list of wrongs to be avenged, as you will see.

After the traditional kiss, the happy couple marched down the aisle to the strains of "Saved at Last, Saved at Last." It was time for the reception in the lower section of the church. Having been in the bland basement once before, I was surprised that so little decoration had been used for the festivities. There were no extra angelic wings floating about. It was all rather austere. Guess they spent so much time making wings for the members of the wedding ceremony, they didn't have time for the ambience.

The bridal couple was at the bottom of the staircase as the guests descended. Rosemary was in a completely different mood. That marvelously winning smile of hers was stretched to its limits, and she simply beamed with victory—or should I say, *happiness*. Whatever it was, she had what she wanted, and she was content. Just think: It only took one brother to calm the evil spirit lurking in that church.

When we passed the wedding cake, Mother said softly to the members of her family, "Oh, if only they would have let me buy them a cake!" One look at the cake was all it took to understand what she meant. It was obvious that the cake was homemade and decorated by an amateur. An attempt at making little wings out of frosting had failed completely. One could only hope that the bride would cut quickly into the monstrosity. Fortunately, Charles was not behind me, so I did not hear his comments about the confectionary wonder. After passing the cake, our family sat down at a nearby round table.

It took quite a while for all the guests to assemble for the reception. Charles helped us pass the time with his observations of various aspects of the ceremony and the decorations. Even

Mother forgot that she was heartbroken when Charles said, "I really thought Rosemary would fly in instead of walking." Aunt Lucy tried stopping him, but he carried on until the happy couple came for the cake-cutting ceremony. Charles said, "If it tastes like it looks, pass the pepto." Aunt Lucy whispered something, and Charles responded, "I'll get the recipe for you, Mother." We all laughed.

Our amusement was under scrutiny, but we had not noticed. When I looked at the cake table, I saw Rosemary's dark eyes concentrated on us. I caught my breath. There went another mistake for her list of retributions. I could not have been more correct, as you will see.

Grape juice, unfermented of course, was served with the cake. Charles asked for champagne when he went for the beverage, but the lady who was passing out the punch gave him a look that wiped the smile off his face. He returned to our table and said, "This is more of a funeral than a celebration!" But Charles was to make another mistake much more serious. When Mrs. Shane made her round of the tables, Charles asked, "Where is the happy couple going on their honeymoon?"

Mrs. Shane's face stiffened. "Oh, such a thing is not in the Jesus Plan. We would not waste time on treating ourselves to luxuries. No, there are souls to be saved, and that's where we spend our time after marriage."

Charles responded most indelicately. "Well, I can think of something better to do after getting married." He laughed and looked at us, but Mrs. Shane raised her head heavenward and walked away. Again, Aunt Lucy reprimanded her son.

The reception was short, and guests began leaving after the Reverend had given another long prayer and the cake had been cut and distributed. There were still two hours before the dinner, so Charles suggested that we have a drink somewhere. Everyone agreed, and we followed Charles, whose talent for sniffing out a tavern was well-known.

When we entered, Charles placed Jim between him and me so that his youthful age would not be noticed. We were soon seated in a leather-walled establishment not far from the church. Charles said, "I'd need to know that this place was close if I was a member of the Jesus Plan." Aunt Lucy rebuked him again, but she laughed with us too. She knew that her son had only begun. His wit kept us amused the whole time we were there. When a cute waitress came over, Charles flirted, as usual. Aunt Lucy told him to behave, but the server was used to such attention and teased him back. After a few remarks, Aunt Lucy and Father both spoke up. Fun was fun, but naughtiness was out of line with such company. Charles agreed and apologized. The time flew by, and we were then off to the dinner, which was being held in a restaurant owned by a member of the church.

We entered The White Dove and were escorted to a large round table for eight. Since there was six of us, we wondered who would join us. Charles said, "I hope it's not our two newly married angels." It was not. Reverend Shane had arranged for a fellow minister to join us. It was a great mistake. Mr. Shane escorted an elderly couple toward our table. The Reverend Trits was tall and skinny, and his suit was really for a shorter man. His wife was quite robust, with a bust of such proportions that I was afraid of what Charles might say. When they reached us, Mr. Shane introduced them most earnestly. "Please give me the pleasure of presenting to you two of the most God-fearing people I know. Their ascension some day to heaven is assured. They are among the chosen workers of God."

Charles immediately commented, "I do hope we are worthy of your presence."

Reverend Shane frowned but walked away. Reverend Trits bowed his head and said a prayer. Charles looked at all of us and raised his eyes heavenward. Yet there was nothing we could do but lower our heads and hear another blessing. When the man finished exorcising our table, Charles asked him, "Are you also a minister in a Jesus Plan?"

Such a comforting voice responded! "Yes, I have been chosen, and I am thankful to serve our Lord."

"Where is your church?" Father asked.

"In Peoria, Illinois," Mrs. Trits replied. "It is a new congregation, and it is growing quickly under my husband's guidance."

Such humility! I thought. *Bet their hellfire system works well in an economically depressed town like Peoria.* I then asked the minister, "When you said that you were chosen to serve the Lord, who chose you?"

Mrs. Trits again answered, "Why, God, of course!"

"Yes," Reverend Trits agreed. "It was the most momentous moment in my life. I'll never forget it. I was standing under an oak tree when I heard a voice call me out for work in the Lord's pasture."

I remembered something from a history class and said, "Standing under a tree seems to be the place to be if you want communication with higher powers." Both Trits looked at me with suspicion. They could not figure out whether I was trying to make a joke, or whether I had a point in making such a statement. I relieved their minds by continuing, "I'm referring to the fact that Lord Buddha sat under the Bhodi tree and received eternal wisdom."

After the slightest hesitation, Reverend Trits said, Oh, yes, of course. But he was a pagan."

That startled me, but I continued, "Well, millions of Buddhists would not agree, but that's not important."

"What is important?" Mrs. Trits asked, testing me.

"In my opinion, I think it is very important in this day and age that the great religions of the world should unite."

The Trits looked blank, as if they could not even think of a comeback. Finally the Reverend asked, "Why?"

"Since you ask, I feel obligated to expound my theory. Globalization has changed our world, not only economically but socially. We know each other better every day. Yet the world is so divided into religious groups, our species will end up fighting among ourselves if we don't assimilate the great religions."

"That's preposterous!" Mrs. Trits commented and looked at her husband as if they were sitting with the "wrong kind."

The rest of the family was amazingly quiet and allowed me to respond. I said, "Perhaps, but it's our only salvation. The world is becoming a country of one, so we should expect turmoil and conflict until we have settled the answer of God."

The Reverend, alarmed, asked, "What do you mean, 'the answer of God'?"

"Which way shall we worship God—as we Christians do, or as the Muslims do, or as the Jews do, or as the Hindus do? Or should we join them all together?"

"Why . . . why . . ." The Reverend was speechless.

Mrs. Trits leaned over and said something to her husband. He nodded and then said to all of us. "My wife is not well. I'm afraid we'll have to excuse ourselves. Please forgive us."

"Oh, we're very sorry," Mother said. My father repeated her expression, but we knew he wasn't sorry.

"I do hope you're feeling better soon," Aunt Lucy added.

The Trits stood and began leaving the hall. Reverend Shane noticed that his friends were leaving and quickly ran to them. We could not hear their discussion, but the Trits were escorted to another table at the far end of the building.

Charles said to his mother, "Did you have to be so kind? She's only sick in the head."

"And look," I said, "they're not even leaving. Was it something I said?"

Charles laughed loudly and patted me on the back. "Congratulations. Not only were you saying some very interesting things, but you also got rid of the Trits. I'm proud of you."

"Tom," Father said, "I've heard you express most of those opinions before, but I found it especially interesting that this time you suggested that the religions all become one."

"Yeah," Charles added. "You've not wasted your time at school this year, and it shows."

Mother and Aunt Lucy started a soft conversation between themselves, but the latter winked at me. I am sure that she was glad that the haughty Mrs. Trits had left the table.

"What's globalization?" Jim asked.

"Tom will tell you later," Father responded. "Dinner is on the way."

A serving girl with an angelic expression brought two plates of baked chicken and foodstuffs and put them in front of Mother and Aunt Lucy. They remarked about the pleasant aroma and the attractive display. Charles, in the meantime, was busy winking at the server. She returned with two more plates and almost spilled them while trying to look at Charles. He laughed, and she turned away quickly. When she brought the last two plates, it was necessary for her to step between me and Charles. I saw his hand going down to pinch or pull, and I quickly slapped it. Charles laughed again as she hurried away. Jim also noticed and laughed.

Aunt Lucy said, "Charles, you've caused enough trouble today. Behave!" Then she whispered to Mother, but I heard it: "If I didn't love that son of mine, I do believe I'd shoot him."

"Oh, Mother, that cute little serving girl loved it!" Charles blurted out, defending himself.

"I think she did," I added, smiling.

At that moment there was a noise from the cake table. Rosemary had set a plate down very hard. She was looking at us while the serving girl was talking with her. The vampire's eyes glistened.

"Let's finish our dinner," Father said.

Unfortunately, Charles' behavior became another item on Rosemary's list of grievances. I guessed later that the longer we stayed, the longer the list grew.

Driving home, Father asked me about the theory I had expressed during dinner. I confessed that it was partly based on a lecture I had heard at the college from a visiting physicist. I just took his thought a little further than he proposed.

Mother said that she did not comprehend how religions could merge, and Father said it was daydreaming. I put forth a rebuttal. "Our species has little time before the disaster sets in. Radical Muslims are way ahead of us. We'd better start working on unification now!"

"Too fantastic," Father replied.

"But my darling Tom, surely you still believe in God?" Mother asked meekly as if she were afraid of my answer.

"Mother, dear," I responded, "how could anyone look at the pictures from the Hubble telescope and not realize that there is a higher force than we have even contemplated? No religion even matches it."

"So you do believe in God," Mother said anxiously.

"Of course, Mother. Call it what you wish. There is a higher power, and we simply have not comprehended it completely.

Maybe we never shall, but we can recognize our limitations. We can fully understand that as we are, we are heading for oblivion. Nothing can stop the oncoming religious wars except unification, a realization that we are all one. Remember, demographics show that Europe will be Muslim by 2050."

"You're making me sleepy," Jim exclaimed. "None of it makes sense."

I laughed. "Well, Charles thought it was interesting. Pity that it upset the Reverend Trits."

"He's a numbskull," Father said.

"Yeah, he made me sick," Jim added.

Father continued. "Charles gave us some good laughs, but his behavior was improper. I'm sure Rosemary did not appreciate the laughter at our table."

Mother changed the subject. "Oh, I wish we could have brought John home with us."

We became quiet, and no one said much the rest of the way.

Two weeks passed before we heard from the newlyweds. Mother had made a couple of calls to the church, but the messages she left on voice mail went unheeded. At first we were very disappointed, but after a few days a normal routine was established, and we did not talk about the new daughter-in-law quite so much. Yet I had the feeling that Mother was thinking about her son all the time. She did not seem as cheerful as usual and kept very busy.

When John did call one morning, he asked if he and his wife could drop by that evening. Mother immediately invited them for dinner. He accepted, and Mother revived in spirit. We were all rather anxious for their visit and agreed with everything Mother instructed. There would be no questions about religion or anything concerning that "strange theory" of mine about the unification of religious faiths. Since we knew that Rosemary would say grace at dinnertime, I could hardly believe that the feared subject would not be mentioned. I was correct.

That evening we were waiting for them as usual in the family room. Rosemary entered like a ruling biblical queen. If she had worn a cape, it would have flown open as she came in with her pet slave behind her. Mother hastened to greet them, and

Rosemary bent over and kissed her neck. I thought that she was going to bite her, but it was a kiss. Who kisses on the neck? Well, vampires, of course, but then John did the same thing. Mother looked at him rather peculiarly but then smiled and welcomed them "home." The rest of us made our hellos as the couple came in and settled on the couch.

John had great news. A member of the Jesus Plan owned a series of warehouses throughout the state. He had asked John to be a manager of one in Peoria, Illinois. It was just the sort of work that John had done in the military, and he was excited. "I'm starting at the top, thanks to the Jesus Plan," he exclaimed. Everyone congratulated him. "So you see, there was no need for me to go to college. I'll make more money now than I would with a degree."

"But John, wouldn't it be—" Mother hesitated. She saw Rosemary's eyes becoming brighter and wider. "Well, if that's what you wish," she continued, changing her tone, "we'll be happy for you."

Rosemary sat up straight and spoke as if making an announcement. "John will be very successful. He is in the Jesus Plan, and nothing can stop him now."

Father congratulated him, and Mother smiled, showing her contentment. I wanted to say something, but withheld it.

Jim did ask, "How does the Plan help him?"

Rosemary's dark eyes turned on Jim, and he looked away. Then she sweetly said, "Jim, you're too young right now to understand. When you are a little older, your brother and I will help direct you to the Lord's divine way."

If I had had a raspberry horn, I would have blown it. The nerve of that bitch! It was so obvious that she was demeaning me. She considered me too lost for help. I did not protest. There was no point, and Mother was biting her lip.

"Let's have dinner now," Mother said joyously. "John, you escort your wife into the dining room. Isn't this exciting, everybody? Our son has brought his wife home for the first time."

The family moved into the dining room.

"When will you be moving to Peoria?" Father asked as we sat down.

"Later this month," Rosemary answered.

"Oh, what a shame," Mother said kindly. "You were given a house near your church, and now you must move."

John spoke up. "There is one of our churches in Peoria. You met Reverend Trits at the reception. He's the minister there."

Smiling, Mother replied, "Oh, how nice for you to already have that connection."

"Yes," Rosemary interjected, "the Trits will be a great asset for us. They are very highly respected in the Jesus Plan. His sermons are just brilliant."

I noticed that Mother was sort of holding her breath, so I said nothing.

"And better yet," John added, "he has already told me on the phone that he and Mrs. Trits will help us find a place to live. Isn't that wonderful? Everything just seems to be going great."

Rosemary looked down at us from her perch and said, "That's what being in the Jesus Plan can do for you."

Since relations were strained after the episode at the table, I said, "Well, Jim and I are planning on going to a movie this evening. We're sorry that we're leaving on your first visit since the wedding." Fortunately, Jim did not say anything, he only looked surprised.

John said that it was all right, but Rosemary did not respond, nor did she look at us when we left.

Mother told me the next morning that the newlyweds expressed great concern about my developing philosophical outlook. Rosemary warned my parents that I was on the wrong path and that her father had found my theories to be blasphemous. Mother said that she had defended me and had assured them that I still believed in God. Rosemary had said that the fires of hell awaited me if I did not repent.

I said, "Mother, that woman's a menace. She's like something from medieval Spain, sort of a Grand Inquisitor. What right does she have to judge others? Isn't that a no-no in the Bible?"

She answered, "Tom, it's too complex for me. I just want us to be happy and to believe in God. His love will save you, I know."

I decided that there was no point in upsetting Mother. She had protected me from the vampire as best she could, and yet she was still fearful for my well-being. I did not want to cause her concern, so I said, "Thank you for defending me, Mother. You know I love you." I gave her a hug and a kiss on the forehead. She went about her housework quite content.

A week later, some more surprising news came from the newlyweds. Rosemary was in the hospital again. Mother, Father, and I rushed down to St. Agnes and met with John in the waiting room. We were informed that the daughter-in-law had suddenly developed pains in her abdomen. When medicines would not help, John had taken her to the hospital where she was being thoroughly examined. He was afraid that an operation would be necessary, which the doctors would soon verify.

"Oh, you poor boy," Mother exclaimed.

"Let's not worry now, Mother," John commented. "We just do not know anything yet."

Mother sat down, and we followed her example. I looked through the magazines but found nothing worth reading. After a short while, a doctor came in and said that Rosemary was being taken to the operating room. He would report back as soon as they knew anything. Father and I thanked him, but John had already succumbed to tears and leaned on Mother's shoulder.

"Don't worry, darling," Mother soothed as she patted his shoulders. "We'll help you all we can."

We sat quietly with only an occasional insignificant question. No one said much, because we were afraid of bringing up a subject that would be hurtful for John. I especially stayed silent, because I was sure that my brother had been well indoctrinated about the spurious nature of anything I might bring up for discussion. Well, I would not want to upset the Jesus Plan anyway, so I looked at a pointless magazine.

After two hours, the doctor returned. He asked John if he could talk in front of the rest of us, and my brother agreed. The doctor explained that they believed that there was a growth in his wife's uterus, which might be cancerous. John closed his eyes and said, "Oh, no!" The doctor continued. "We must ask your permission to operate. It could mean a hysterectomy. Mother bit her lip. She knew it meant that there could be no children, but she said nothing. John agreed to the operation, and the doctor left.

We all sat down again. Father sat on one side of John and said that he would pray for Rosemary. Tears came to John's eyes, and he put an arm around him. Mother sat on John's other side and tightly held his hand while she prayed. I walked up to my brother put a hand on his right shoulder. "John, our whole family prays for you and her." He looked up and thanked me as tears ran down his cheeks. Perhaps we had never been so close before.

Unfortunately, Reverend and Mrs. Shane arrived. When they heard the news, they fell on their knees and started praying. John joined them, and they prayed for a miracle. After some time, Mrs. Shane sat down by Mother and said, "It's so sad. If it's true, Rosemary will never have children."

Mother became tearful immediately. I'm sure she wanted to scream, "I told you so!" but she retained her composure.

Reverend Shane discounted his wife's remark. "We don't know if that's true and there could be a miracle. Let us pray for one." Again he was on his knees, and John and Mrs. Shane joined him.

I could not stand any more prayer. If that seems irreligious, I do not care. I'm just sure that the heavenly computer has more to do than register the same darn prayer over and over. I went out for a Coke or coffee.

About five in the evening, the doctor returned. There had been complications, but he was sure that the patient would survive. "Halleluiah!" the Reverend cried out, and to our embarrassment, he fell on his knees again for prayer. John and Mrs. Shane, of course, joined him. It made me sick.

The doctor paid no attention to those in prayer, but turned to me and said, "She is now in the recovery room and will be sleeping through the night. I would advise you to go home and rest. Come back in the morning when she'll be recuperating." His suggestion was greatly appreciated. When he left, John looked up at us and said, "It's a miracle! Her survival is simply a miracle."

I stated that the doctor was probably very experienced with such operations and that Rosemary had probably had expert care.

"No!" John insisted. "It's a miracle!"

Reverend Shane agreed and prayed most earnestly in prayerful tones. Mrs. Shane had taken a seat because the hard floor hurt her knees, but she prayed with the others all the more.

Mother, Father, and I looked at each other. I shrugged my shoulders. Mother put her hands on her son's shoulders and patted him. John looked up and said, "Yes, Mother, it is a miracle. You don't understand the Jesus Plan. I prayed for a miracle and it came."

"If you say so, my darling, that's fine," Mother said kindly, continuing to pat him.

"I think we should go," Father commented.

John stood up and continued talking. "You can't understand, because you aren't ready yet for such understanding, but I know it was a miracle."

Reverend Shane agreed and assured my parents that in the future they too would find meaning in prayer.

"We do pray, Reverend," Father interjected, "but we never make a public spectacle of it."

The Reverend and Mrs. Shane looked at my father as if they had seen the Holy Ghost. Father did not care. He too had endured enough and escorted Mother from the room. I followed, wanting to laugh.

My laughter was short-lived. The next day there was a scene straight from hell. The three of us returned to the hospital. Fortunately, the Shanes and John had not yet come. Rosemary was awake, and we were allowed entrance to her room on arrival. She saw us and looked away. Mother approached her bed and said, "Good morning, dear. I hope you feel rested."

The wrinkled, evil-eyed creature turned toward her and snarled, "As if you cared! You hate me because you think I can't have children, but I'll show you. I've got the power of Almighty God on my side, and I'll show you."

Mother tried comforting her. "My dear, don't excite yourself."

"Don't call me 'dear,' when I know you don't mean it. You see, I understand you better than you realize. You were against our marriage, and now you're gloating that you were right! Well, you're wrong. I shall have children."

Mother was in tears and wiping her eyes. Father put his arm around her and led her away. I went up to the bed, but the scorpion was waiting for me too. Her eyes were blazing, and her mouth was twisted in anger. "So, you've come to gloat too! Well, let me tell you something. The fires of hell are burning bright for your horrible insults to the living Christ. He has condemned you to eternal damnation."

I was so taken aback, I could not speak; but when I realized that it might be the only chance I would ever have for rebuttal, I said, "May God forgive you!"

"You dare to call on God!" she screamed as I walked away.

Turning in the doorway, I looked back and made the sign of the cross over her bed.

I am sure that the scream she let out was heard at the end of the long hall outside her room.

A nurse came running in, followed by a doctor. I watched as they rushed to her bedside and tried to calm her. She yelled, "Get him out of my room."

The doctor told the nurse to get him a hypo, and Rosemary snarled, "Don't try to put me to sleep. I want him out of my room!"

John and Reverend and Mrs. Shane entered as I quickly left.

Naturally, we did not see John for a couple of weeks. Mother's inquiries to the Shanes received rather cool replies. All we really knew for some time was that the hellion was recovering and then finally released. When John did come to see us, he was not the son that had left our home. He tried shaming us for causing Rosemary's outburst at the hospital. We did not argue. He would never have considered our explanation of that dramatic scene. We took the blame because we understood what he wanted. So we apologized. It calmed him down somewhat, and we had a fairly pleasant visit.

Mother asked about Rosemary's present condition, and John replied that she was up walking around and would be at church the next Sunday, where her absence had caused much sorrow among the parishioners.

"That will be wonderful for her and you," Mother said.

"Yes, it will," John replied. "I can't tell you how much she contributes to the services." Mother nodded.

"When do you now plan on moving to Peoria?" Father asked.

"Very soon, I think. Reverend Trits has found us a house near his church, and we're making arrangements for the move."

"I'm so happy for you," Mother said.

"Have you seen the warehouse where you'll be working?" Father asked.

"Yes," John responded in a much more pleasant mood. I drove down there and looked it over. It's a fine distributing facility. I'll be doing what I did in the army, so it should work out very well."

"That's fine, John," Father said.

"Will you be able to come and have dinner with us before you depart?" Mother asked.

John frowned, but said, "I will try. It depends on how Rosemary is feeling."

"Of course," Mother said and then humbled herself. "And let me say again how sorry we are that we disturbed her so at the hospital."

I felt like shouting, *Don't give in to that vampire!* But I controlled myself, not wanting any argument.

John said he would tell her our sentiments, and he was sure that the greatness of her mercy and the kindness of her great heart would allow her compassion. "So she will probably be most glad to see you before we leave."

If I could have puked at that moment, I believe I would have. John was sounding like Reverend Shane. On a Sunday two weeks later, John called and said that he and his wife could drop by for tea in the afternoon. Mother cancelled attending an event in our church so that she could have them over. It made us anxious, but there was no way to refuse seeing them if we ever wanted relations with them again.

That afternoon Mother prepared some cookies for our tea with the newlyweds. Jim made plans to visit a friend. When he left he said, "I don't want to see that vampire!" No one objected; we all felt that way. So once again, Mother, Father, and I waited in the family room for the arrival. Mother had prepared a tea table near the fireplace. The cups, lemon, and cookies were ready. "Wonder what sort of mood she'll be in," I said.

So the moment arrived. The newlyweds drove up the driveway in the new car that my parents had bought them. They parked and came toward the house. Looking out the window, I reported that Rosemary did not look dour. My parents sighed with relief.

The couple came into the family room with smiles on their faces. Rosemary was all charm. So charming, in fact, that the three of us were afraid to approach her. She went to Mother first and took one of her hands and held it. "My dear mother-in-law, I am so glad to see you."

Mother gave a forced smile. I think she was not sure whether the creature was preparing her for a bite or a kiss.

It was the latter. The vampire leaned over and kissed Mother's forehead, not her neck as I assumed she would. Then she said, "We just had to see you before we left for our new home."

John seconded the idea. "Yes, we would not have left without visiting you."

Rosemary continued. "We must thank you for all the nice things you've given us. I love my silver set, and John is very happy with the new car."

"Yes, Father," John again seconded the idea. "It's a dream, and I'm sure we're going to enjoy it more and more."

Mother and Father seemed relaxed and asked everyone to sit down. I was the only one who seemed to notice that I had not been greeted, but of course I did not care. As the couple were taking their seats on the couch, John looked over at me and said, "Hi, Tom." He did smile, but she did not even turn toward me. I reasoned that angels weren't supposed to associate with the damned.

The afternoon tea visit was stultifying. If my parents and the visitors had been manikins, the conversation could not have been more stiff and boring. I was allowed a word or two, but I tried to keep out of it. By nodding or shaking my head, I acted as if I was part of the repartee, but inside I was yawning. No one was being truthful. Rosemary still loathed us and, in a sense, had come merely to gloat over her victory. She had won the prize, my dear brother, and she was relishing her conquest to the ultimate. I pray that I never have to endure another afternoon tea like that one.

When they left, we knew that we had said a final good-bye to our son and brother.

Chapter 6

The Miracle

A month later John called from Peoria. He was coming for a visit because his company was sending him to Chicago on business, and he was looking forward to seeing us because he had great news. Yes, a miracle had occurred, and he could not wait to reveal it. Neither could we wait to find out what it was. I suggested that Rosemary had sprouted wings and was flying higher than Amelia Earhardt. Mother did not care for my analogy. She reprimanded me because she wanted no arguments when John came. I promised to behave. However, I later overheard Jim say that he thought the miracle might have something to do with sex. He laughed and said, "They finally did it!"

Mother was taken aback. Her youngest son was thinking about the forbidden "that?" It is well-known that we Christians made sex a bugaboo in the Middle Ages. Fortunately, in our time we are slowly accepting it. However, in our family, it was still not a topic for discussion. She called out, "Jim! Aren't you ashamed?" He shook his head but the matter was dropped.

When John arrived and came bursting joyously into our family room, we were in awe, because he was not the gloomy young man we expected. Then, when he spoke, we were startled. "Mother, you're going to be a grandmother!" he said. "Isn't that wonderful?"

Mother was so traumatized by his news and reaction that she stuttered for perhaps the first time in her life. She had assumed that Rosemary was not capable of childbirth after her operation. "But—but really?" she asked.

Father helped her out. "John, that's great news! When did you find out that Rosemary is pregnant?"

Then came the revelation about the falsity of his claim. "No," John laughed. "We've adopted a family!"

"What do you mean?" Mother asked.

"Legally?" Father inquired.

"No, but we now have three children. You see, a family moved into a small house by our church. Rosemary met them and was enchanted by them."

I wondered what the children thought about Rosemary.

"So," John continued, "when we found out that they did not have a church, we invited them into the Jesus Plan. They accepted right away. It made us so pleased that we just took them under our wing."

"What does that mean?" Mother asked.

"Well, we help them with things. Like the little girl needed a coat, so we bought her one. The two boys needed clothes too, and we gladly helped them out. Rosemary is constantly going next door to be with her new family. The children even call her "Mom," and that thrills her."

"You must be doing very well at the warehouse," Father said.

"Yes, I am. The owner has practically doubled my salary because I quickly straightened out the big mess he had there. It was just the same sort of stuff I did in the army."

"That's great, John," Father complimented.

"And you, Mother, now have your grandchildren. I can't wait for you to meet them. When can you come for a visit?"

"Oh, John," Mother exclaimed. "I can't tell you how happy it makes me to see you so content."

John looked at me, and I nodded as if I too thought it was just fine, but I did not. If there is one thing I've learned in life, it is that a white lie in society is an absolute necessity for survival.

"We'll come visit anytime you invite us," Father said.

"Great!" John exclaimed. "Well, how about next weekend?"

"That would be wonderful," Mother responded.

"Rosemary will be so glad to see you," John said.

So everyone calmed down. The miracle had been revealed without a star in the sky, and we were set for a visit with our new relatives: three grandchildren and their parents. I wondered about the latter. What kind of people would take charity so easily? Fortunately, the next weekend Jim went to a summer camp sponsored by our church. Father told me that when he dropped Jim off at Mr. Miller's, the minister said he would keep a close eye on him. He said he didn't want us to lose another son and then gave a short chuckle. Father was rather taken aback by the remark, but told me that he did not respect Miller's intellect anyway, so it did not matter. Father added that at least Jim would be away from Rosemary's den of iniquity. I laughed.

Our drive to Peoria was on a lovely summer day in June. It was very pleasant, and we did not talk much about what we expected. Yet we all three were anticipating another dilemma. We were correct. When we arrived at the address that had been sent to us, we were astonished to find children playing in the yard of a rather run-down wooden house. The grass had many weeds and needed cutting. It did not seem the best place for the children's toys. A boy of about eight stopped bouncing a ball and stood looking at us. His younger brother continued playing with a tricycle, and a little girl about the same age was holding a plastic dog. "There are your grandchildren, Mother," I said and laughed. *And what a mess they are. They all need a bath, and I'll bet my brother bought those toys.*

"Oh my. Now what?" Mother said.

We drove into the driveway, and two of the children came running to the car. John came out of the house and gave Mother a hug. After shaking hands with Father, he introduced them to their new "grandchildren": Mike, the oldest; then Ricky, who had not left his vehicle; and last, the little girl Susan, who showed

Mother her doggy. Mother could only smile, and the children did not know what to say. "You'll love them," John said to Mother and started leading us toward the house.

Out of the door and onto the porch came the ruler of our destiny. Rosemary was in an apron and all smiles. She came down the steps and asked Mother how she liked her new grandchildren. Mother smiled and said, "Oh, they do look like sweet children."

"They are," Rosemary assured her. "And they've already started Bible classes in the Jesus Plan."

Big surprise, I thought.

At that moment, however, I did receive a surprise. Rosemary looked at me and said, "Oh, we didn't know that Tom was coming."

There was an awkward moment, so I asked, "Should I leave?"

"No," said John, "you can sleep on the couch."

That was good news, of course, but Rosemary never seconded the idea or said anything to me. She picked up little Susan and placed her in Mother's arms. "Now, darling, you say hello to your grandmother!" The child only stared, and Mother handed her over to John. "Well," Rosemary commented, "she'll warm up to you. Let's go into the house."

It was obvious that the house was part of the Jesus Plan. There were pictures of Christ-related themes on each wall of the living room. I saw the worn-leather, rickety couch on which I would be sleeping and wished I had not come. John brought the children inside, and I asked where their parents were. "Oh, since today's Saturday, they are in the adult Bible class at the church. We'll join them this afternoon."

"Why don't I stay here and look after the children," I suggested, glad that I had so quickly found an excuse to be free of their Bible studies.

"That's a great idea," John replied. He turned to Rosemary, who had not heard me, and said, "Darling, Tom can stay with the children this afternoon when we are at the church."

Rosemary turned and looked at me. I felt a short shudder. I knew she did not like the idea. She could only say, "We'll see." Then she invited us to be seated.

"What sort of work does the children's father do?" Father asked.

"Harry works in my warehouse, and their mother, Hilda, works in a school cafeteria. They're hard workers."

So, we had been introduced to the new branch of our family. It was then that I received my appellation. "Mike," John said, "show your Uncle Tom your new game!" The boy sort of wrinkled his lips as if he did not want to be bothered, but he picked up a box and brought it over to me. It was a Bible puzzle with a picture of Jesus, which he had not yet started putting together. When I asked him if he would like me to help him start the picture, he shrugged his shoulders. John said to him, "Now, you answer your uncle Tom."

I felt sorry for the boy, but he looked up at me and said, "Okay."

The door opened suddenly, and the children's parents came in. We were introduced to Harry Moots, a well-built, nice-looking young man and his wife, Hilda, a short, plump woman who had a most ingratiating smile. Rosemary came from the kitchen and asked, "Harry, did you get the order?"

"Yes," Harry responded, "and I must thank you from the bottom of my heart for getting those chairs for me. They'll be perfect with the table I'm building."

"Harry is an excellent carpenter," Rosemary told us.

"Yes, he is," Hilda agreed, smiling profusely. "He's made most of our furniture, and Grandmother Rosemary found the most precious lamps for us."

Grandmother Rosemary, a new appellation that made me want to puke, answered with such a sweet smile. "Now, Hilda, you know the Lord will provide!"

And John will pay for it, I concluded.

The vampire then told us the schedule for the day. We would have a small lunch and then go to the church for the Bible study program. John, to his wife's dismay, interrupted and reminded her that I would watch after the children while the adults were in class.

"Do you really think that's a good idea?" Rosemary asked. "We could ask one of the young ladies in the angel preparatory class to keep them."

"Oh, I don't mind." I said. "I'll read while they play."

"Sure," John agreed, and the matter was dropped. However, I noticed that Rosemary gave her husband a look of "you'll be sorry!" During lunch, she took Mike aside and whispered with him. He nodded. I assumed she was giving him instructions for the period he would be with me. I found out later that I was correct.

When the adults finally left for the Bible study, the children stayed with their games and me. I sat down with a magazine, and the children were busy with their toys. To my surprise, Mike brought his Bible puzzle over to me and asked if I would like to help him. I agreed, and we went to the kitchen table.

While sorting the pieces, I asked him, "Do you like having an auntie like Rosemary?"

He looked at me rather confused. "She's not my auntie; she's my grandmother. She's also my guiding angel."

I sort of laughed, and the boy smiled for the first time. "And how do you feel about having a guiding angel?"

"Well, she's awfully bossy."

I laughed, and he joined me with a broad smile.

"Does she do nice things for you too?"

He nodded and said, "Yes, I have a new set of blocks and things. She gets them for me if I go to Bible class with her."

"Does she get your sister and brother nice things too?"

Mike nodded. "But I get the most."

Don't worry kid, their turn's a-coming.

"Do Daddy and Mommy also get nice things?"

He nodded again and said with enthusiasm, "Oh, yes. Daddy got a new big television, and Mommy got a new stove."

"Do they have guiding angels too?"

Mike thought for a moment. "I guess so, but usually my angel helps them."

"You've got quite a helpful angel, don't you?"

He nodded.

"What did she whisper to you in the kitchen before she went to Bible study?"

"Nothing much, but she doesn't want me talking about Jesus with you."

What one can learn from the mouth of babes! I smiled and said, "Then we'll not talk about Jesus, okay?"

He nodded.

While the parents and the guiding angel were away, Ricky was content playing with his new tricycle. He was hitting the furniture occasionally, but when I would look in on him, he only smiled. His sister spent her time talking with her plastic dog, which she called Bow-Wow. I asked her if she had a doll, and she just looked at me. Mike explained that she was not allowed to have dolls because—he hesitated and then said, "Well, just because."

"Perhaps the guiding angel doesn't like dolls," I nonchalantly mentioned.

Mike nodded.

What in the hell is wrong with a little girl having a doll? I asked myself.

By the time the adults returned, Mike and I had put together Jesus's outline on the kitchen table. Rosemary came in and said to me, "Your parents are walking back. It's quite close, you know, and it's a beautiful day." Then she noticed the table. "Oh, I forgot about the puzzle. Did you talk about Jesus while we were away?"

"No," I replied.

The guiding angel looked at Mike and repeated the question. The child stiffened but shook his head. I wondered, *What would have happened if he had said yes?*

The vampire was not content with our answers, but she seemed powerless to make a scene out of it. So she declared "rest time," and the parents began preparations for taking the children home. They collected toys and had short conversations with the guiding angel. I heard phrases like, "I'll get that tomorrow!" and "When does she need it?" *Another giveaway program,* I decided.

After the other family had left, I had a chance to ask Rosemary why the little girl Susan was denied dolls.

She snapped back, "How do you know that she can't have dolls?"

"Mike told me when I asked her if she'd like one."

Rosemary was heating up. "Why did you ask her?"

"Well, I thought it would be nice to give her a gift while we were here." I humbly replied.

"No, she doesn't need a gift—especially a doll."

"What's wrong with a doll?" I asked.

John entered at that moment and heard my question. Rosemary looked at her husband, and he interceded for her. "In the Jesus Plan, we don't allow the popular sex education that is ruining children in our schools."

"How does a doll come under that subject?" I asked.

"A child might ask were the baby came from," Rosemary answered.

"That would take a rather precocious child, but what would that matter?"

Rosemary's Evil Eye began concentrating on me. "We don't want to instill unwanted interests in a child until it is of an age to understand."

"You mean sex?" I asked.

"Well, of course!" John replied, looking sort of sheepishly toward his wife.

"I've never heard of a child being affected by a doll. Besides, holding a doll is surely good for a little girl who will someday be a mother."

"This is enough!" Rosemary commanded. "I won't let you contaminate our children."

"Well, you'll make a lesbian out of her, you wait and see."

The vampire stood up and glared at me. "John," she almost howled, "are you going to let him talk like that in our home?"

John took the offensive. "Tom, one more remark like that, and you will not be welcome here anymore."

I raised my hands as if I surrendered.

My parents returned, and we all took a rest. Later we went out for dinner in a restaurant owned by Mr. Turner, a member of their church. He was a straight-faced, overweight man who looked like a leftover from a wax museum. It was like meeting a brick wall. Yet, because we were joined by the Trits and Rosemary, a pillar of the church, he insisted on saying a prayer for us after we were seated. I did not groan, but Mother said later that she thought she heard one. I think she was expecting one from me.

Whatever, I stifled my conversation and listened to John, Rosemary, and the Trits as they discussed church matters with the proprietor, who was constantly coming to our table with another idea. Seems there was a problem as to where the pulpit should stand in the main hall of the church. "It needs to be in the most auspicious place," Mr. Turner kept insisting. After several interruptions about the pulpit, I almost told him where to put it, but fortunately I was able to control myself.

The dinner was rather mediocre because the vegetables were cooked almost beyond recognition. It finally ended, and we were able to escape another of Mr. Turner's theories about the pulpit by going out when he was busy in the kitchen. How disappointed he must have been when he came back into the restaurant and found that we were gone. Still we were stuck with the Trits. Fortunately, they did not come home was us, because Reverend Trits was going to practice his next-day's sermon with Mrs. Trits. "I always read it to Mama," he said as they left. That explained her mummified brain.

It was a terrible night. After the evening prayers, we all retired. The couch was not made for sleeping, so I did not sleep much. I kept worrying about that little girl who was denied dolls. I'd never heard of anything so silly. She was allowed animals, so I supposed it would make her a veterinarian. I was glad when the sun came up.

After breakfast we prepared for Sunday services in the Jesus Plan. I had earlier sworn that I would never again enter that angel refuge, but I was caught. For Mother's sake, I agreed to attend. I decided that I would make the sermon a sort of game. I would keep track of how many pathetic interpretations Reverend Trits made.

He kept me busy. We were seated near the organ again and could appreciate the blasts that were made when introducing a new section of the service. Again the organist played songs that we had never heard, except for one. "Walk with Jesus" had been used in the wedding ceremony. However, the version sung in the Twits' church was especially long. I think the walk covered Christ's forty days in the desert. Whatever, the time for the sermon finally came.

Reverend Twit chose to read 1 Peter 4:12 for his Bible quotation: "Beloved, do not think it strange concerning the fiery trial which is to try you, as though some strange thing happened to you; but rejoice to the extent that you partake of Christ's suffering."

I sat there wondering, *If God created us, why did he create suffering? Is it some kind of game He plays? Does the heavenly computer allow each of us just so much pain? Why didn't He create a more perfect human in the first place?*

The Reverend went into his sermon. "Trouble is common to man, but it reveals the moral fiber of our souls. Have you ever seen a golf course without hazards? They are part of the game! Golfers speak of courses with the most hazards as the most challenging. Trouble creates a capacity for handling it."

So, this life of ours is a game of the gods! The Greeks were right. We're stuck with eighteen holes to go through. Well, Dostoevsky said that he'd just as soon pass back the ticket, because he doesn't like the ride!

I couldn't take any more. I turned off the sermon and just contemplated whatever I wanted. There was no doubt in my mind that I was named correctly. I am definitely a "doubting Thomas." But what's wrong with that? I sat there thinking of other things and passed the time feeling much more content than I would have if I'd listened to the wisdom of Reverend Twit.

After the sermon and another blast from the organ, we sang another song before we went into the lower section of the church for a reception. Harry and Hilda sat with us. The latter exclaimed, "Wasn't that a brilliant sermon?"

Mother agreed, being kind.

Father nodded. I'm sure he hadn't listened either.

Before Rosemary and John could join us, I turned to Hilda and said, "I was surprised that you don't allow your sweet little Susan to have dolls."

Hilda was surprised by the question but came back with, "Oh, the church doesn't allow it."

Mother was quite surprised and asked, "Why?"

Hilda had no answer, but she was saved by the arrival of Rosemary and John. When the vampire heard that we were discussing the education of children, her eyes burned and she blurted out, "The Jesus Plan is the proven way for a successful and happy life. Our children learn from the beginning what is right and wrong."

Nobody dared contradict her, and I had promised not to argue. So the matter was dropped. Luckily, the reception started. We had coffee and cake brought to us by serving girls. I saw a cute young lady and thought of the waitress that Charles had accosted at the wedding. I had a sudden inclination to pinch her à la Charles, but I figured it would only cause a scene. There was enough pain in the church that day thanks to Reverend Trits.

Later, Harry whispered to me that he too did not yet understand why a child should not have a doll. I whispered back, "Well, you'd better stand up for your rights now, or it will be too late!" His face showed his surprise at my answer.

Reverend Trits came downstairs and went to the center of the large hall. He made announcements and also introduced our family to the small audience. My parents were presented as the loving and caring people who had reared their fine, new member John Whitney. The guests applauded. The minister then tacked on, " . . . and their son Tom," but before I received an accolade, he continued with the announcements. If he had planned to hurt my feelings, he'd made a mistake. In fact, it only showed how rude and lacking in etiquette he was. When he finished, he and Mrs. Trits made a round of the tables and then stopped at ours. We said some niceties and then explained that our return home required that we leave. There was much hugging and kissing, but I was able to avoid it by walking over by the coffee urn as if I wanted more. Then there was the final prayer, and our family managed to exit.

Rosemary and John accompanied us to our car. Rosemary asked Mother, "Did you have a chance to say good-bye to your grandchildren?"

Mother smiled and said, "They're so sweet. I gave them a hug."

"Be sure to send Christmas gifts when the time comes," Rosemary said. She looked at Mother rather severely. "They *are* your grandchildren now."

Of all the nerve! Then she turned to me.

"Did you like your niece and nephews?" the vampire asked in a tone that seemed to be threatening me.

I did not care and said, "Yes, I liked them. They told me a lot of things I found very interesting."

"What did they tell you?"

"Mike did mention the lovely gifts you've given to his parents. I think that was very charitable of you!"

Her blood pressure must have hit a record. She turned red, the way I suppose a vampire could after a good bite in someone's neck.

John left Father and came over by her. He asked, "What's the problem?"

Hearing the word *problem*, I thought of the Reverend's sermon. Without thinking, I said, "Oh, nothing. Just one of those things that Reverend Trits was talking about this morning. I'm referring to the kind of problem that God gives us to improve our character."

Rosemary let out an "Ohhhh" and walked away.

John looked at me and said, "Aren't you ashamed, upsetting someone who cares so much for you?"

I almost gagged at that, but I said, "John, what are you talking about? I don't think I upset her. Just ask her."

Rosemary had gone to the other side of the car and was talking to Father. John walked over there, but he did not dare interrupt her. Her face was red as a beet, and she was saying something. I entered the car and heard, "Good-bye, now. I'll help your grandchildren write to you. Keep in touch!"

Father and Mother said they would, and she started waving as we backed out of their driveway.

When we drove off, my parents asked what had happened. Mother said, "I've never seen her so mad."

"Well, Mother, it's like this," I explained. "She's developing another family for John. We'll lose him completely now."

"Oh, dear," Mother commented. "My darling boy! What will his life be like?"

"Miserable," Father said. "He'll be paying for those children for the rest of their lives. Gold-diggers like Hilda and Harry never give up when they've found a sucker."

"You should have heard what little Mike told me while you were in church. John bought all of those toys that were thrown around everywhere."

"So that's what it was all about," Mother said.

Father added, "I'm afraid John will be paying for that family the rest of his life, and I think she's done it for vengeance. She knows we did not want the marriage, and she's working now to break off with us completely. You'll see."

Our drive home was silent. We were depressed, and we wished we had not gone to Peoria. For several days we avoided talking about our unpleasant weekend spent with our lost family member.

Jim returned from camp and wanted to know all the details about our visit in Peoria. So we started telling him things that we had tried to forget. Mother gave her version, and so did Father. Jim was glad he'd stayed away. However, when he and I were alone, he told me that I was responsible for his having a terrible argument at camp. I asked, "Why?"

"You talked about globalization and how it was affecting religions—as well as the financial aspect. The camp director did not agree, and I couldn't defend myself. He got very upset and said I was a blasphemer."

"Jim," I responded, "you have to learn that there will always be people who will not agree with you, no matter what the subject is. You must realize that what you were espousing is a new concept, and it affects the beliefs of people. They don't like that, and many have gone to their deaths rather than to accept changes in their faith. During the Spanish Inquisition in the sixteenth century, it was common for people to be burned alive for refusing to retract a disagreement with the church. The Spaniards even drove all the Muslims out of Spain, because they refused to accept the Christian faith. This is the problem today. Religions must join together, but they aren't capable of changing their traditions."

"But which religion has to change?"

"They all do and, of course, they can't."

"Why?"

"Because of what I said! They don't want to change their established position. They are right and everyone else is wrong. It will lead to disaster."

"When?"

"Maybe not in our lifetime, but it's coming. You see, because the world has shrunk—that is, because of modern technology—we know each other better now. God's message of peace on earth and good will toward men is in every faith, but people don't want to change their own interpretations. Who is right? Is it Moses with his commandments? Is it Christ with his offer of eternal life? Is it Mohammed with his paradise? Is it Krishna through reincarnation? Is it Buddha? Their followers are all right in their own minds, so it's God against God. That will lead to perdition."

"But they all don't teach the same thing," Jim commented.

"They all preach one God. There's got to be some means of compromise, or the species will destroy itself through war, pestilence, and hunger."

Jim suddenly asked, "What about the Jesus Plan?"

"That's just a fluke created by ignorance. Our dear sister-in-law uses Christ as an evil weapon for her own self-interests. That church uses the Bible out of context for its own aims. Rosemary is one of the mainstays of such an establishment. Her ignorance is frightening. She has dominated our brother because he's like most of mankind. People want to be led. Dostoevsky pointed that out. If you take the chains away, people are lost. Rosemary has given John strength by binding him to her own creed of self-satisfaction. It's dangerous. Should something happen to her, he would be lost. It's sad, but true.

"She's sucking the life out of him," Jim said.

"Unfortunately, he likes it. He doesn't have to think. That's mankind's problem; it's weak and wants direction. So it gives in to anything that provides a sense of security. Poor John, he'll always be trapped in her ignorance."

"It's too much for me," Jim said. "I'm going to bed."

I laughed.

Chapter 7

Finita la Comedia

For several months the family was kept together by Mother's weekly call to the Jesus Plan in Peoria. John would sometimes answer and talk briefly about the activities that were keeping him so busy, but other times she would have to leave a voice mail message, which would not be answered. At least we were in contact, and that gave my parents some satisfaction.

Then, to our surprise, John called one hot August day and said that he would be stopping by after a business trip in Chicago. The whole family was delighted. However, when he came, we were astonished. He had gained weight and did not look well. His eyes had red streaks and he walked slower. In the course of a few months, his health had deteriorated. When we commented about his change, he made light of our concern, saying that he still felt very well. He did say that he had been terribly busy and maybe that was slowing him down a little. Mother ushered him into the den, and we all followed, settling into our customary seats to hear what he had to share.

There was unpleasant news. Mrs. Shane had passed away and was buried in a cemetery near their church. Mother instantly asked why John had not informed them earlier. He explained that Rosemary wanted a very private funeral in the style of the dictates of their church, which outsiders would not understand. He did say that he'd wanted to call us, but she was adamantly against it. That we could well imagine. However, there was one pleasant aspect of her demise. Mrs. Shane had left Rosemary a hundred thousand dollars, which they had placed in an annuity for the future.

"That's smart thinking, son," Father said, nodding his head.

"But couldn't we have helped you?" Mother implored. "Or at least sent flowers?"

"Rosemary felt that you shouldn't be bothered, since the Jesus Plan funeral is a little different from the usual burial."

Yeah, I thought, *they shoot them to heaven via cannon.*

"How is it different?" Mother asked.

"They speak in tongues around the coffin and then around the grave. It's quite different from what we're used to." Before anyone could ask another question about it, John continued. "However, I do have some other sad news. Rosemary is not well again."

"Oh," Mother exclaimed. "You poor boy!"

"What's the trouble?" Father asked.

"We don't know yet, but she is going to have some more tests this next week. That's why I'm not staying overnight. I must get back to the airport."

"What a shame," Mother sighed. "I was looking forward to having you in your old room. It's still there."

John smiled and moved toward her for a hug.

"John," I interjected, "I hope you'll keep us informed."

"Sure, Tom," he replied. "You know how she loves you all."

I held my tongue. *Yeah, she loves me so much that she wanted you to kick me out of your house!*

Mother wanted to prepare a lunch for us, but John said that he simply had to catch his plane. "There's only one late-afternoon flight to Peoria. I flew in on the morning flight yesterday, and now I must go home. She'll be expecting me."

"Of course," Father and Mother said almost together. The latter added, "Jim will miss seeing you. He's gone on a nature trail with his friend Joe."

"Tell him I said hello," John replied as he stood up to leave.

The family gathered around him. It had been a short visit, but somehow there seemed to be a little of the old familiarity that we'd held in common in the past. It was as if the prodigal son of the family had returned after being away a long time. As we walked with him out to his rental car, Mother asked about the grandchildren."

"Oh, they're all right," he responded, but he didn't go into any details. I thought that was odd and wondered if some of the luster in the relationship was wearing thin.

"How is Reverend Shane taking the demise of his wife?" Father asked.

"Oh, he's secure in the Jesus Plan. It has its own way of handling things."

"Please give him our love," Mother said.

John smiled and sat behind the wheel of the car. Mother put her head through the window and kissed him and Father reached in and gave him a hug. We all waved as he drove away.

Walking back into the house, Mother said, "Oh, my poor John. It's just as I thought it would be. She'll be sick all their lives."

"You know," I said, "it was strange that he didn't say much about that family. I wonder if they've realized how Hilda's taking financial advantage of them."

"I'm more concerned about Rosemary's health," Mother inserted. "It doesn't sound good."

"That's her hold on John," I said. "She uses her health and her great Plan to keep him pinned down."

Mother reprimanded me. "Now, Tom, be fair. That's not kind."

Father remained quiet but winked at me when he went inside. I knew he agreed. That woman would use anything to hold John. It was just another of her means of separating him from our family. The fact that she kept her own Mother's death from us showed her lack of respect. I found myself hating her again.

Several days went by, during which Mother worried constantly about John, not about Rosemary. She did not even think of sending flowers. It proved that Mother also felt that her son was being victimized by that woman. Finally John called and said that his wife's condition was very serious and that she had been operated on. The doctor had found a cancerous tumor in her innards, and he feared that the disease had spread. Rosemary was now in a private room recuperating. Father asked if we should visit, and John said that we could if it was convenient. Of course we made plans.

The next day, Father drove the four of us down to Peoria, where we went directly to the church. John was at the hospital, so we hastened there. In the waiting room, he was asleep while seated, leaning back against a wall. Mother put a finger to her lips, not wanting us to awaken him. We had started out of the room when he called, "I'm not asleep. Please come back." We had awakened him, but he was very glad to see us.

"John, you're not looking well," I said to him. "I don't think you're getting enough rest. Your eyes are bloodshot, and you've gained more weight."

He confessed. "I'm not getting enough sleep, but I've been very busy."

"How can we help you?" Father asked.

"Your being here is very kind. I do appreciate it," he said. He gave Mother a hug and shook hands with his Father and brothers.

I thought John should probably talk with a doctor, but I wasn't sure he'd take my advice. I expressed my feelings to Father, and he agreed. John shook his head. "No, I'm fine. I just need some rest. I'll do that when she's better."

"When can we see her?" Mother asked.

"This afternoon. She's having some tests made now. It will take a while."

At that moment, Reverend Shane came into the room with his withered face looking very dour. He walked over by John and shook hands with Father, but not with me, as if I cared. Mother expressed her regrets about the loss of Mrs. Shane, and that brought on a long prayer right in the middle of the waiting room. *How gauche!* I thought, but he rambled on.

The waiting was unbearable. Reverend Shane lectured rather than talked. I became bored, so I took Jim out for a soda. When we returned, the family decided that we would have lunch in the hospital cafeteria. Reverend Shane stayed with John, and that was a relief. When we returned to the waiting room, we were told that Mother and Father could see Rosemary. They went with John to her room, but when they came back, they seemed downcast. John said, "She's asking for you, Tom."

That surprised me, but I went with John down the hall to her room. As we walked along, I had a strange feeling that something extraordinary was going to happen. I even felt a shudder. At her door, John told me that she wanted to see me alone. When I entered her room, I was startled at the sight before me. Rosemary was as pale as the sheets on her bed, and her large eyes were closed. At first I thought she had died.

As I approached the bed, one of her arms rose, and she grasped my hand. Her eyes opened, and she looked steadily into mine. Her voice was so weak that I had to lean over her to hear. "Tom, do not try to change John. He is on the Jesus Path, and it will save him and comfort him. You must not interfere."

"Why do you think I would?" I asked softly.

"Because you are Ishmael personified. There is no hope for you, and you must not drag John down into hell with you."

I was astonished at what she was saying. I hardly knew how to react. It suddenly came to me that she knew she was dying. These would be her last words to me. I finally came out of my bewilderment and said, "Rosemary, it is the time for truth. You have used the Jesus Plan for your own selfish reasons. You have made John into a puppet, and you control the strings."

Her mouth opened, and she whispered in a hoarse, ugly voice, "Get out, you fallen angel."

"No," I said. "You were trying to make me fear God's judgment, but you've failed. I will take John from your grasp and revive his life."

She gave a soft moan, then said louder, "I curse you!"

"No," I replied. How I had the nerve to say the following to a dying woman, I do not know, but the words poured out of me with ease. "The cursed cannot curse another. John will be free of you, and you will freeze in hell!"

Where she found the energy to yell as she did, I don't know. But she let out a chilling scream that quickly brought John running into the room and to her side. She said to him, "Get him out of here. He is damned!"

"What?" John asked, confused.

She yelled louder, even though it must have taken almost all the strength left in her body. "Get him away! He is accursed forever!"

I left the room, quite shaken. I had not expected such rancor or such a scene. I leaned against a wall. *Had I really said those things to that dying woman? Why? Should I have just taken her abuse and said that I would not harm John? Yet I could not. I wanted her to know that she had failed. Christ was not to be abused the way she had used him.*

When my brother came out of the room, he asked, "Tom, what happened in there? Couldn't you keep your far-fetched ideas away from a sick woman? Why did you argue with her? She so peacefully asked to see you, and you upset her terribly. Why did you do it?"

"She started it, John, and I'll tell you someday, but not now."

"I don't know how I'll ever reconcile you two again," he said as we entered the waiting room.

He must not know that she's dying! I thought.

Harry and Hilda and their children entered soon after us. Little Ricky ran up to my Mother and said with hesitation, "Hello, Grandma." Then he looked at his mother as if he sought approval for the way he did his little act.

Mother was surprised, but she bent down and picked him up. "Oh, isn't he a sweetheart," she said, turning around for all to see.

Hilda introduced her children to my younger brother, calling him Uncle Jim. He did not like that appellation, and instead of fawning over them, he brusquely nodded.

We visited awhile with our new family, but our purpose for the visit had been accomplished. Even though it meant driving into the night, we returned home. There was no way we could help John, and we felt it would be easier for him if we were not on his hands. He finally agreed and said that he would report about her condition every day. We said our good-byes with hugs and handshakes. Jim was disappointed because he did not see Rosemary—not that he liked her. He was just curious about her.

The next morning after the long, tiresome drive, the family slept in. About nine o'clock, we started gathering in the sunroom for breakfast. Jim asked Mother, "Do I have to be called Uncle Jim by those brats?"

"Well, if we are going to please Rosemary, I guess we'll have to put up with them. I find the arrangement rather uncouth."

"It's rather silly actually," Father added. "Rosemary's doing it merely to spite us. She's terribly cunning."

"I don't think we'll be bothered by them much," I said. "We probably won't be visiting there very often."

Mother said, "But she expects me to send those children presents at Christmas and on their birthdays. John gave me a list with the dates."

Father coughed. "Well, really! No, I don't think we're going to get caught in her game. We'll not do it!"

"But for John's sake, I fear we must!" Mother counteracted.

I spoke up. "Well, we've lost John, so I see no reason for doing what that hellion wants."

Mother shook her head. "No, no, my darlings! I'll never give John up completely."

One evening a week later, we were sitting in the family room, when an owl suddenly called out from the woods surrounding our house. "What a haunting sound that is," Mother said. "I hope it's not an omen of bad news."

"Don't be so superstitious," Father said. "It's just an owl."

The next day, John called. Rosemary had passed away. We were never able to convince Mother that her daughter-in-law had not visited us the night before. "The owl had called her name!" she insisted and would believe nothing else.

There were many strange aspects to the demise of the unusual daughter-in-law. She had left explicit instructions on who could attend her funeral and what would be done in the service. It would be held in her father's church not far from us, which was convenient. Also, she had ordered the monument. John told us that Jim and I were not to attend, but Mother and Father could if they wished. I assumed that my last meeting with the vampire had excluded me. It was certainly a relief to me that I was left out.

When Mother and Father returned from the funeral, they had disturbing news. The Moots had moved in with John. It was one of Rosemary's last wishes. John told Mother that the children were running around like crazy, and Hilda did not seem to correct them very often.

Mother was sure that it was driving her son crazy. She was terribly worried about his health. She reported that he had gained more weight and looked very, very tired. "He is working too hard," she said, "and that family is draining every penny they can out of him."

Father spoke up. "The thing I found most distasteful was that Rosemary had a large tombstone created that had John's name already engraved next to hers. He told me that she'd made him promise that he would never remarry, because the Jesus Plan does not allow it. That way she and he will be together in heaven. That is one of most screwball ideas I've ever heard!"

"The funeral service took forever," Mother continued, "because they allowed personal comments from members of the church congregation. That church certainly does have a strange burial service. People talked in strange languages and sort of danced by the coffin. It seemed rather impolite to me, but they carried on their silly rites even at the graveyard."

Both parents were terribly distressed by what they had seen and experienced by merely going to a funeral.

At this time, communication with John became difficult. If Mother called him, Hilda or Harry would answer, and Mother never found out what she really wanted to know. Sometimes even Mike would answer, and he could never answer a question.

Calls to John's office were usually recorded on voice mail and then not answered. Mother worried constantly.

A month after Rosemary's demise, Mother and Father began making plans for their fiftieth wedding anniversary. Mother was finally able to contact John and invite him for the occasion. He promised he would come because he had three days' leave available at that time. My parents were delighted and the family planned various activities that would make him feel at home. Mother was inviting members of his high school football team for the anniversary dinner so he would have friends with him. Jim even said that he would take John to a baseball game—John's favorite sport. There was no doubt that the family was at ease in making plans. We knew that the vampire would not be with him.

When the great day of his arrival came, we were shocked at his appearance. His stomach protruded over his pants, his eyes squinted continually, and he was dressed rather shabbily. His worn-out jacket had pulled threads in the sleeves, and he did not wear a tie. Father thought that he looked worse than he had at the funeral. He seemed morose. Everyone noticed the change, but he did not complain. He hugged Mother and shook hands with the rest of us. We thought we would cheer him up by telling him some of the plans we had made. He would nod his approval, but he did not show any enthusiasm. He did not seem to be the John we knew and loved.

"She's still got him entrapped," I whispered to Father.

"He's suffering," he replied.

Mother tried to be cheerful around him, but she was very worried. For his first dinner at home with us, she prepared his favorite meal. Only after it was over did he comment about how pleasant it was to have sauerbraten again. It made Mother very pleased, but he did not mention the special apple pie, which he ate with gusto. He was still not his old self.

The next day, the anniversary party took place in a country club that my parents sometimes visited. They were not regular members but, through a friend, had the privilege of using the club on special occasions. It was not a large party, but being with three of his old high school buddies did entertain John, and he seemed relaxed and amused. Mother was very pleased. Yet many of the guests told John that he did not look well. He would deny it, but the frequency of the comments caused him to retire early. The next morning, Father suggested that John see the family doctor, but he made light of the suggestion.

That afternoon, Jim took our brother to a baseball game in the city park. John had played there himself and enjoyed seeing the field again. Jim reported that John had cupped his hands and yelled several times when he was not pleased with a particular play or if he saw someone he knew. Jim thought he had enjoyed the game.

After they returned from the game, John told me that he would like to talk with me for a minute. We went out into the sunroom. He explained that he had an annuity of considerable cash, but Rosemary had made him put Hilda Moot's name as the beneficiary. He was planning to add my name to it so that I could pay for his funeral when the time came. I scoffed at the idea of worrying about a funeral at our age, but he said that he was merely informing me of his intention. He had already told the Prudential Insurance Company of his plan, and my name was being put on the beneficiary list. I thanked my brother for the honor but said I considered it rather premature. He smiled.

After dinner we rested in the family room. It seemed like old times. Our conversation was mainly about the anniversary party the evening before. John told us about the activities of his high school friends, and Father shared some of his memories. It was a pleasant evening. When John walked past my bedroom, he said, "Goodnight, Tom," as he used to when he lived with us. The world seemed right.

A few seconds later, I heard a terrible noise in John's room. I thought it was strange because there was no furniture that could fall over and make a noise like that. I ran into his room, and he was lying on the floor, holding onto his bedspread and trying to breathe. I yelled down the hall for help, and the family came quickly. Father immediately called for an ambulance. Mother knelt down beside her son, but he was gasping for air and could not talk. She was soon in tears. Fortunately, the police ambulance came in just a few minutes. The men asked my parents and Jim to leave the room. Then they released John's hold on the bedspread. Two other men brought in a hammock, and they placed him on it. I asked if I could go along, and they agreed. In the ambulance they began working on him immediately. Our family gathered in the waiting room of the hospital. Finally, a doctor came and informed us that John had suffered a severe stroke and was not regaining consciousness. Everything that could be done was being done.

John passed away in his sleep.

Our family went from joy to grief in one day. Father said, "She would not let go of him." We knew what he meant. Rosemary's curse had followed him and worn him down. Her evil grasp had been a determined one. She would possess him forever.

It was then that I had an idea for a final victory over that horrible woman. Why should we honor her desire and bury my brother beside her? True, it would be unconventional not to place him beside her in their plot under the monument that she had undoubtedly designed. But why should we allow her that final victory? *No,* I concluded, *we would not!*

After consoling Mother, our family retired for the night. No one slept well, but the next morning at breakfast I revealed my plan. "My dear parents and brother Jim, I have an announcement. First, I want to mention that Rosemary caused us much grief. She took our brother away and used her satanic forces to subjugate him to her will. We all sensed that there was something strange in that woman, and we even called her a vampire. She was a *psychic* vampire. She overwhelmed John's mind through her insane interpretation of Christ. Jesus did not want us to be biased, prejudiced, and selfish like she was. She used Him to make a shield around John—a force he could not overcome. She was horribly ignorant, but she was incredibly cunning. I think you all agree with what I've said."

"Yeah!" Jim exclaimed.

"She was strange," said Mother, wiping away her tears.

Father sighed and looked askance.

"She was a vampire," Jim burst out and laughed.

"Well, are we going to let her have a final victory?"

"What do you mean?" Father and Mother both asked at the same time.

"Are we going to bury John beside her like she wanted? Remember, she made him promise to lie beside her so they could be together in heaven."

"But they were married," said Mother.

"Yes, but we don't have to give her the final victory of having what she wanted. We'll put him in the cemetery here with our grandparents."

Everyone was quiet.

I said adamantly, "I will not give that ignorant, evil woman a final victory over us. John will not lie beside her for eternity."

Mother started crying. "Oh, how sad!"

"Tom," Father said, "we've got to think about this. It's highly irregular."

"But it's no one's business but ours, and I'm going to see to it that she is not victorious. I shall even go to her grave and tell her."

"Oh," Mother exclaimed as if frightened. "Do be careful."

I laughed. "Yes, you would think that she could reach out of the grave and grab you. But she won't. I shall defy her."

"I'll go too!" Jim exclaimed.

I laughed and said, "No, Rosemary hated me the most, and I want the pleasure of defying her one last time."

Mother and Father finally agreed that I could carry out the funeral and burial arrangements. When I told Reverend Shane of my plans, he was horrified and fell on his knees to pray. Well, he could have stayed there forever, for all I cared. I did what I wanted. I had John cremated and arranged a simple funeral in our family church. I told Mr. Miller that his sermon could not be more than five minutes. He chuckled.

Then came Rosemary's final efforts at vengeance. When I called the Moots, Hilda answered. I explained what had happened, and she said, "Rosemary gave me some papers at our last meeting. She told me to open them when she passed away. I did, and it seems that she left me an annuity."

I told her that I knew about that, but that my name had been placed on the beneficiary list too. She said that my name was not there. I replied that I would check, but that I only wanted enough money for his funeral. She hung up the phone.

Then I realized that I had been correct. The Moots were only gold-diggers and were bleeding my brother for money. I was sure it had contributed to his demise. I believe that money so begotten is accursed.

Aunt Lucy and Charles came for the funeral. It turned out to be a rather festive occasion, more of a wake than a solemn service. For some reason, the entire family felt relief. They realized that John was no longer in the grasp and control of that selfish woman, and they rejoiced at his liberation. He seemed to be with us, and we had a merry time at the post-funeral dinner. Charles was in top form. He made many witty jokes about the vampire and what her reactions would be to their merriment. Even Mother enjoyed his wit. He recalled Rosemary's behavior when he remembered certain encounters with her. "I'll never forget," he said, laughing, "How upset she got when she saw the naked *Sun Singer*! I was so disgusted I wanted to expose myself."

Aunt Lucy and Charles departed, and our family settled down. We were facing a new life. Brother John had been an integral part of our plans and joys, but now he was gone forever. New plans were to be made. We were a family of four.

It was now time for my visit to the grave of the vampire. It was not a long drive, and I chose to do it at night. At the beginning of this report on the alien creature that had come into our lives, I gave you some details about my trip to the gravesite. Now, you may know what I told her.

When I stood before the grave, I said aloud, "Rosemary, I have come to inform you that you were not victorious after all. I have had John cremated, and he is at rest in our family cemetery." Suddenly there was a frightful noise. Had an owl shrieked in the distance, or was it a vicious snarl from the grave? Whatever, it disrupted my talk, but I continued. "You have abused Christ's message to mankind for your own selfish interests. Your incredible ignorance has allowed you to subvert the meaning of the morality that man is capable of." Suddenly and unexpectedly, it seemed that a vision of Rosemary appeared standing on her grave.

A soft, but unpleasant-sounding voice said, "You are damned!"

I spoke back. "No, you are accursed. You are to lie in your cold wasteland forever without him. John is free. No longer can you use your evil ways to dominate my brother. Flee, you fiend from hell!"

My illusion slowly disappeared. There was an incredible quiet around me. The moon shone brightly through the trees. I instantly felt a sense of release. I had not only freed my brother from his tormentor, but I had liberated myself.

May all who endure the desecration of Christ's wisdom be acquitted.